"We've got to get out of here."

McKenzie heard the terror in Alex's voice. Even in the waning moonlight trickling into the caved-in tunnel, Alexandra Vance was beautiful. The way her full lips moved, the fear in her eyes, touched him as nothing else had since that horrifying—

He savagely shut down his thoughts. Taking a deep breath, he whispered, "We aren't going anywhere."

Her eyes rounded. "Why not? I'll die if I don't have surgery soon!"

Her cry of desperation triggered the entire terrifying sequence, and he was snared in the grip of the nightmare once again.... Adrenaline poured through his bloodstream, and his heart started slamming against his rib cage. Sweat bathed his face.

"Look," he began in a rasping voice, "I can't ever go back. Do you understand? I don't want to let you die, but I can't go back."

Dear Reader,

Welcome to Silhouette **Special Edition** . . . welcome to romance. Each month, Silhouette **Special Edition** publishes six novels with you in mind—stories of love and life, tales that you can identify with—romance with that little "something special" added in.

April has some wonderful stories in store for you. Lindsay McKenna's powerful saga that is set in Vietnam during the '60s—MOMENTS OF GLORY—concludes with *Off Limits,* Alexandra Vance and Jim McKenzie's story. And Elizabeth Bevarly returns with *Up Close,* a wonderful, witty tale that features characters you first met in her book, *Close Range* (Silhouette **Special Edition** #590).

Rounding out this month are more stories by some of your favorite authors: Celeste Hamilton, Sarah Temple, Jennifer Mikels and Phyllis Halldorson. Don't let April showers get you down. Curl up with good books—and Silhouette **Special Edition** has six!—and celebrate love Silhouette **Special Edition**-style.

In each Silhouette **Special Edition** novel, we're dedicated to bringing you the romances that you dream about— stories that will delight as well as bring a tear to the eye. And that's what Silhouette **Special Edition** is all about— special books by special authors for special readers!

I hope you enjoy this book and all of the stories to come!

Sincerely,

Tara Gavin
Senior Editor
Silhouette Books

LINDSAY McKENNA
Off Limits

Silhouette Special Edition

Published by Silhouette Books New York

America's Publisher of Contemporary Romance

To all of the women
who served in the military during the Vietnam War—
your help also deserved medals that you were never given.
I salute you.

SILHOUETTE BOOKS
300 East 42nd St., New York, N.Y. 10017

OFF LIMITS

ISBN: 0-373-09733-6

First Silhouette Books printing April 1992

Printed in the U.S.A.

LINDSAY McKENNA

spent three years serving her country as a meteorologist in the U.S. Navy, so much of her knowledge about the military people and practices featured in her novels comes from direct experience. In addition, she spends a great deal of time researching each book, whether it be at the Pentagon or at military bases, extensively interviewing key personnel. She views the military as her second family and hopes that her novels will help dispel the "unfeeling machine" image that haunts it, allowing readers glimpses of the flesh-and-blood people who comprise the services.

Lindsay is also a pilot. She and her husband of fifteen years, both avid "rock hounds" and hikers, live in Arizona.

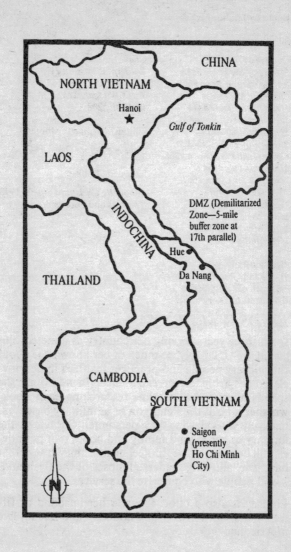

Chapter One

South Vietnam, April, 1965

"*We're hit! We're hit! Prepare for emergency landing!*"

Alexandra Vance gasped as the pilot yelled the warning. The marine helicopter suddenly shuddered, a hail of bullets slamming through the aircraft's thin skin and peppering the cabin. She gripped the nylon seat as the aircraft jerked upward. Its engine shrieked and groaned, the blades flailing awkwardly, like wings on a wounded bird. The crew chief gave a startled cry, gripped his chest, then crumpled to the deck. The smell of hot oil stung Alex's nostrils as the door gunner began returning fire, and the pounding *chut, chut, chut* of the machine gun reverberated through Alex's body like pummeling fists. Black, oily smoke spewed up in front of the cockpit's shattered Plexiglas windshield. Directly above where Alex sat, the pilot and copilot worked feverishly to keep the helicopter airborne over the enemy jungle.

Like the crew, Alex wore a helmet, the wire jack plugged into the intercommunications system. Curses, screams and groans filled her ears as the world seemed to shatter around her.

Oh, God! Alex cried out involuntarily as bullets smashed through the cockpit again, striking behind and around her. The gunner screamed and was catapulted backward. Alex threw her hands up to protect her face from flying debris. She was being wrenched from side to side as the aircraft bucked and lurched drunkenly. One of the pilots slumped forward, struck by a bullet. Without warning, fire and shrapnel exploded through the cockpit.

A hot, stinging sensation seared Alex's shoulder, and she was slapped against the bulkhead by gravity as the helicopter wrenched downward. Heat scorched her, and she gagged and choked on the nauseating smoke filling the cockpit. Then the aircraft nosed over, its engine still shrieking like a wounded person.

Everything began to reel off in single frames, as if Alex were viewing a movie—only it was a movie in which she was the main participant. The seat belt held her captive as the Sikorsky helicopter brushed along the tops of the triple-canopy jungle. The trees acted as a last-moment cushion to the crippled aircraft, so instead of nosing down and grinding with savage, killing impact into the red earth of Vietnam, the helicopter caught in the trees as its airspeed bled off.

The helicopter was on fire, with smoke funneling out of the cockpit and escaping through the open rear door near Alex. There was a great screech as it listed unexpectedly, its tail flipping into the air as it settled on its starboard side, finally halting.

Alex hung suspended upside down in the cabin, the nylon seat belt nearly strangling her. Frantically, she looked around. No one else moved. Her heart denied that her companions might be dead. Alex clawed wildly at the metal clip. Her gaze locked on the machine gunner's window—her only escape route. Brush, leaves and limbs had collected in the usual exit area during the helicopter's long, downward slide. The window was partially blocked by the vegetation.

Fire and smoke, too, continued to pour into the cabin as Alex struggled with shaking fingers to release the safety harness. Suddenly the belt gave way, and she fell hard against the aircraft wall below her. Panicking, she flailed blindly around to check the crewmen who lay unmoving at her feet. Anxiously, Alex tried to find pulses on their necks, but her desperate fingers felt nothing. Coughing and choking violently, she tried to make her way forward to the cockpit to see if the pilots were still alive and needed help escaping, only to be driven back by the flames and intense heat.

Her eyes blinded with tears as she groped her way through the dense, thick smoke, Alex fell onto wobbly knees. Which way was the window? She couldn't see a thing. Heat scorched her skin. *Die! She was going to die!*

On bloodied hands and knees Alex crawled toward the rear, trying to find the exit. There! Her hand met the leaf-and-branch barricade. She lunged through the window. A scream caught in her throat as she threw herself from the burning helicopter, thinking the ground must be nearby. But she fell a good twenty feet, before slamming onto the damp, leaf-strewn floor of the jungle.

Panting to regain her breath, Alex groaned and rolled onto her back. Tears ran down her smudged cheeks as she struggled to move. Directly above her, the helicopter burned furiously, a huge column of black smoke drifting lazily into the clear blue sky. She had to get away from the inferno as soon as possible. Rolling onto her hands and knees, Alex crawled shakily away from the aircraft, moving through the thick foliage. Branches swatted at her, stinging her face and bare arms. Her breath coming in huge, ragged gulps, she moved jerkily, without thought. A powerful numbness took over, and she felt oddly detached, as if she were having a bad nightmare.

Alex had crawled nearly two hundred yards from the initial crash site when she heard voices. She pressed a bloodied hand against her parted lips and froze. Shaking badly now, in the aftermath of an adrenaline rush, she sat back on her heels on the jungle floor. *Vietnamese.* They were Vietnamese voices. Relief swept through her. *Rescue!* She was going to be rescued by the friendly forces of the ARVN!

She tried to rise, but her knees collapsed under her and she fell to the ground. Dirt and damp leaves stuck to her face and short brown hair. Struggling, she tried again to rise. Agony spread from her left shoulder like an out-of-control wave of fire into her neck, down her arm and into her chest. The savage pain caught at her breath, and Alex groaned softly, unable to move. She crumpled slowly into a fetal position. For the first time, she examined her shoulder.

Thirty minutes earlier, when they'd left the marine base at Marble Mountain, Major Gib Ramsey had insisted that Alex climb into a dull green, single-piece flight suit, pulling it on over her buttercup yellow blouse and jeans. Now, staring uncomprehendingly at her shoulder for long moments, Alex finally realized the dark stain spreading across the olive green cotton on her left shoulder was blood. Lifting her right hand, she touched the area lightly. It was not the blood of the brave marines who had just died, but her own.

Alex released a little breath of air. Sweat trickled off her face and soaked into the coarse flight-suit fabric. *Wounded. I'm wounded. God…*

The Vietnamese voices grew louder, more excited. Alex lay, unable to move, frozen into immobility by the realization that she had been hit and was bleeding heavily. Her mind refused to work, except in stops and starts. The pain grew in volume while she focused disjointedly on her shoulder wound. As a fourth-year nursing student, she should know what to do. *Think! Think, Alex. What do you do for a bullet wound?* Squeezing her eyes shut to prepare herself for the pain, Alex pressed her hand against her shoulder. Direct pressure on a heavily bleeding injury would stop the flow. Blackness began to dim her vision, and she quickly released the wound, unable to staunch the bleeding under the wave of unrelenting pain.

With a little cry, she struggled into a sitting position, well hidden by the profusion of plants on the jungle floor around her. Dazed, going into shock, Alex stared at her left shoulder. Had she been hit by metal fragments from the explosion, perhaps? Shrapnel? Feeling light-headed, she fell back and rolled onto her right side as numbness spread down her left arm, rendering it useless.

The Vietnamese were all around her. Alex tried to gather her thoughts but couldn't. At one point she saw a young Vietnamese man, armed with a rifle and dressed in black pajamas, pass within feet of her. She thought he was ARVN and tried to cry out, but nothing came out of her constricted throat and dry mouth. He passed by without realizing her presence. Helplessly Alex lay there, barely conscious. She knew she wasn't dead, and finally, after half an hour, her mind cleared momentarily and she realized she was in deep shock.

Nothing in her affluent Virginia background, growing up with Hiram Vance, her famous congressman father, had prepared her for this. Alex had reluctantly agreed to visit her father, who was touring bases and military positions all over Vietnam on a fact-finding mission. He'd said it was safe. *Safe!* Why had she allowed her father to browbeat her into coming? Their relationship was tenuous at best. Alex knew that deep in her heart she wanted her father to like her— love her—as much as he did her brothers, so she had come, against her better instincts. Hoping to heal the widening rift with her father, she had rationalized that flying to Vietnam to tour the bases with him would work as a peace offering to help mend their differences.

Still lying on the jungle floor, Alex began to shake uncontrollably, her arms and legs taking on a life of their own. It was shock, Alex knew, the continuous surge of adrenaline through her bloodstream causing the reaction. Suddenly, a huge explosion rent the air, sending a thundering clap of sound booming through the jungle like the pounding of a hundred ear-splitting kettledrums. The echo was a physical force, pummeling Alex as wave after wave rolled past her. Wincing, she realized that the marine helicopter had just blown up.

Over the next hour, clarity returned slowly to Alex's mind. On its heels came a wall of chaotic and panicky emotions. Finally tears came, leaking down her muddy cheeks. She cried for the marine crew. They were all dead. At Marble Mountain, they'd treated her like a star because of her popular father's influence and power. The door gunner, a red-haired boy of eighteen, had shyly asked for her signature on a sweat-stained piece of paper pulled from one of the pockets of his flight suit. He'd told her excitedly that he collected autographs.

At first, Alex had protested, saying she wasn't famous, just an unknown person in the shadow of her larger-than-life father. But the door gunner, Private First Class Ken Cassle, had gently insisted. Squeezing her eyes shut at the memory, Alex sobbed. The cry jerked through her like a convulsion, and pain flared hotly in her left shoulder to remind her of the wound. Still, she knew, her heart bore an even larger, invisible, wound for those four marines.

As if her brain was stuck on that time frame, Alex couldn't shake the memories of the past hour's conversations and the images from before she'd left the marine air base. Captain Bob Cunningham, the helicopter pilot, was married—the father of two young children. He'd proudly showed Alex their pictures when she'd asked about them. He'd patted the pocket near his heart where he kept them, saying that the photos were his good-luck charm, that they were going to get him home safely to his family. And his copilot, Lieutenant Jeffrey Whitmore, had just gotten married. His wife was expecting their first child. Now none of that crew would be going home alive. Alex sobbed quietly, unable to stop the deluge of loss she felt for them and their families.

By the second hour since the crash, the bleeding in her shoulder had stopped, and Alex drew in a shaky breath of relief. She focused her limited senses on her surroundings. The sunlight, what little there was, had slanted in a more westerly direction. They'd started the flight to the firebase at noon. Alex looked down at the watch on her dirty, bloodied wrist. It was now 2:30 p.m. She sat up and tried to assimilate and understand her own dilemma. Light-headed, she knew she'd lost more blood than she should have. As a nursing student in Washington, D.C., she had seen blood from time to time, but never like this. She tried to study her left shoulder with impartiality. The flight suit was soaked with blood in a large, uneven circle that surrounded her upper arm, encompassed her left breast and reached halfway across her chest.

The wound didn't bleed when she moved, but Alex wasn't about to look under the loose-fitting flight suit to find out why. More important things had to be addressed. Thirsty, her mouth dry, Alex began to look around for a water source but saw none. The jungle teemed with singing birds. The fire that had engulfed the helicopter earlier had completely died out. Only a few trails of ever-thinning black smoke stained the sky. Everything, it seemed to Alex, was returning to normal.

Her heart gave a giant thud at a noise to her left. A Vietnamese, his face intent, held an ugly-looking weapon against his chest, as if prepared to fire it. Alex snapped her mouth shut and tensed. This man wasn't ARVN, or at least he wasn't in the uniform they wore at Marble Mountain. Instead, he wore a black cotton shirt and baggy black pants. Somewhere in Alex's spinning senses, she recalled part of her egress briefing given by Major Ramsey. He had said that men who wore such an outfit were VC, the enemy. Alex remained frozen. Would he spot her? And if he did, would he kill her?

The soldier halted and slowly looked around, his dark brown eyes intelligent, his head cocked, as if to listen for some out-of-place sound among the normal jungle noises. His hands tightened on the stock of the AK-47 he carried. Slowly, he looked down at the leaf-strewn floor.

Alex's eyes went wide. If she moved, she would disturb the top layer of leaves, signaling the enemy. He was only ten feet away. Sweat popped out on her upper lip. All that protected her from his prying eyes

were the huge, graceful green leaves and ferns that
hung like an umbrella around her head and shoulders. A panicked cry started deep in her throat. She
clamped her mouth shut, in that moment understanding what a helpless rabbit must feel like as a fox
stalked it. Would he hear the thudding of her heart?
She could hear it booming in her ears.

The VC quietly moved on. Alex was amazed at the
way the man made no sound at all. Her heart pounding unrelentingly in her breast, she realized that she
had to get away from the crash site. She licked her dry
lips, which were caked with blood. If she left the vicinity of the helicopter, the marines who might rescue
her wouldn't be able to locate her. Yet, if she stayed,
Alex knew with certainty that the VC would find and
capture her.

Which way was Firebase Lily, her original destination? Her father was waiting for her there. She was no
good with directions. Her two older brothers, Case
and Buck, always derided her inability to recognize
north, south, east and west. With a trembling hand,
Alex shoved her hair from her eyes. Which way was
the sun? The triple canopy of the jungle so diffused
the light that she had no real idea. Never had Alex felt
so helpless, so angry at her own incompetence—or so
alone.

Her father had wanted her to join the military as an
officer once she got her nursing degree. Her two
brothers were already in the Marine Corps. But Alex's talents, if she could even call them that, were
aligned with being of service in other ways. Her father had openly scoffed at her nursing aims, berating

her with the Vance family's hundred-year tradition in the military.

Well, Alex thought dully, *I don't want any part of it. I'm not a killer. I don't even like war.* And yet, as she sat there, Alex knew she was in a war. If Case or Buck had been shot down like this, what would they do? Her confident older brothers probably would have dressed their wounds, gotten up and headed for Firebase Lily.

With grim determination, Alex struggled to her knees. Dizziness assailed her. She tried to ignore the thought of how much blood she'd lost. Focusing on a nearby tree, a rubber tree, she saw sunlight high up on the gnarled, twisted trunk. It took several minutes to figure out an easterly direction, for her mind kept shorting out. Firebase Lily lay directly east of Marble Mountain, some thirty miles inland and near the border with Laos, according to Major Ramsey. He'd shown her the flight route on a map pinned to the wall of the headquarters tent.

Her father had always derided her lack of assertiveness. Why couldn't she be more like Case and Buck: aggressive, extroverted and confident? Alex considered herself a plain brown mouse—just the opposite of her brothers. She compressed her full lips. In her twenty-two years of life, nothing had prepared her for this sort of situation. Still, didn't plain brown mice survive even the largest, most aggressive of cats? She could get out of this situation if she used her common sense.

Alex slowly rose to her feet, swayed unsteadily, then anchored herself until her head cleared. She tucked her left arm against her body, cradling the elbow with the palm of her right hand. Only her mother would have any faith in her ability to survive. Alex loved her quiet, introspective mother fiercely. No matter how over-bearing her father became, Susan Vance always seemed able to gently and quietly maneuver around him to get whatever she needed for the family. Alex felt another kind of pain that equaled that in her aching shoulder. What would her mother do when she found out Alex was missing and presumed dead in the Vietnam jungle? Her mother's health was fragile. Somehow, Alex had to hurry and find the marine base so she wouldn't worry.

Standing against a tree, Alex took stock of many things, among them the art of camouflage and of walking silently. VC stalked the area on quiet, bare feet. Alex knew she'd have to walk just as quietly. She didn't dare crash through the brush like a bull elephant, broadcasting her whereabouts. For long minutes, Alex thought about her plan. When she finally took the first step in her white tennis shoes, she tried to imagine herself as a shadow, slipping between the damp, water-beaded leaves of the jungle foliage.

Near the end of the first hour, dizziness halted Alex. She stood hunched over beneath some large banana leaves, pressing her hand tightly against her left arm. Gasping for breath, she tried to soften the sound of the air escaping from her mouth. Once, she spotted a VC, and quietly eased to her knees. She crouched in a huddled position next to the thick, entwined root system of a large rubber tree, and the VC passed without discovering her.

Shakily, she wiped the sweat from her eyes. She looked down at her right hand. It was covered with blood and mud. Walking had caused her wound to bleed a little more.

Just as Alex straightened to resume her journey, a man's large hand clamped against her mouth. A scream lurched in her throat, and she was jerked backward off her feet and slammed to the jungle floor. Blackness rimmed her vision and she felt him straddle her.

Black dots danced in front of her eyes. He gripped her by the throat. Again, Alex tried to scream. Her eyes grew wide as she saw him raise his hand. A long, savage-looking knife blade hovered inches above her face—aimed directly at her. She threw her hands up to protect herself, then fainted.

What the hell? Corporal Jim McKenzie grunted as he quickly released and got off the woman. As he slid the Ka-bar knife into its leather sheath, his surprise turned to instant concern. He'd heard the American helicopter crash hours earlier. He was a recon marine, accustomed to being behind enemy lines, and against his better judgment, he'd hobbled out of his hiding place on a makeshift crutch to look for survivors. Now he glanced around quickly, his hearing sharpened for any VC in the area. He knew all too well that they owned this piece of real estate, lock, stock and barrel. His left leg was encased in a primitive, makeshift splint, and he bit back a groan of pain as he gripped the woman by the collar of her flight suit and pulled her deep into the nearby banana grove. There it was dark and protected, and they would be shel-

tered by the long leaves that hung nearly to the jungle
floor. No VC eyes would find them here.

McKenzie squinted against the gloom as he as-
sessed the unconscious woman. Who was she? The
flight suit she wore had patches identifying a Marine
Air Group squadron, but not her rank. She was small
and fine-boned, reminding him of the sparrows that
lived around his parents' Missouri cabin. Tansy
McKenzie, his mother, fed the little birds hen scratch
and just a bit of cracked corn during the winter, and
she always had a slew of them waiting around for their
next handout.

Jim's gaze moved to her bloodied shoulder.
Wounded. She's wounded. Stymied as to why she
would be in a marine helicopter in the first place, he
pulled the flight suit away from her left shoulder. Her
yellow blouse was rusty with blood. Was she a spook,
maybe—someone from the CIA? Despite her nasty
wound, his gaze moved back to her face. The short
brown hair lay like a sleek cap across her skull. Her
eyebrows were slightly arched, her lashes a thick sable color against her pale skin. Maybe it was her heart-
shaped face that gripped him, or maybe it was the
memory of the tiny sparrows. She was young, perhaps in her early twenties, her nose small, like the rest
of her. Briefly her slack lips captured his attention.
The vulnerability of her full mouth sent a spasm of
yearning through him, but Jim ignored its tug. Their
lives were at stake, and if they were going to get out of
this area alive, he had to give his full concentration to
survival tactics.

He gave her right shoulder a small shake.

"Hey!" he rasped near her ear, not wanting his voice to carry. "Hey! Wake up, gal!" He shook a little harder.

Alex moaned softly. A voice, a man's ragged, low voice, thrummed urgently through her dazed senses. She felt his grip tighten on her right shoulder without hurting her. Her lashes fluttered as she forced her eyes open to bare slits. Alex inhaled sharply. Instantly, he clamped his hand across her mouth.

"Don't scream," he warned her.

Seconds stopped, hung and froze as Alex's eyes widened. The man who crouched over her was dressed in dark green utilities. His face was oval, with a strong chin and nose, but it was his piercing dark blue eyes that frightened her the most. His mouth was thinned, the rest of his face carved with sweaty, muddy streaks and lined with tension. He was tall and rawboned, and the utility cap he wore low on his dark brown hair made him seem to blend into the foliage that surrounded them.

Then Alex saw his blue eyes thaw, grow wide with concern and lose their intent, predatory look. She felt his hand loosen slightly from her mouth, and she could smell his sweat.

"Don't go screamin' on me, gal," he murmured. "I'm an American recon marine. You hear?"

His voice had a Southern drawl to it. And as Alex moved in and out of semiconsciousness, relief flowed sharply through her.

"Okay?" Jim rasped, leaning very close to her, his hand still across her mouth. She had the most beautiful mourning-dove gray eyes he'd ever seen. The pupils were huge and black, and he knew she was in deep shock. When she barely nodded, he eased his hand from her mouth. Her lower lip trembled and he saw tears gathering in her heart-stealing eyes.

Jim placed his finger against his lips in a silent request for her not to cry out or sob aloud. It was a tribute to her courage as she fought her initial reaction and lay quietly as he hunkered over her. Jim placed his hand on her left upper arm, where the material was soaked with blood. He looked around, listening carefully. VC were thick in this neck of the woods, and the odds were stacked against him getting safely back to his tunnel.

Struggling not to cry, Alex closed her eyes and tried to breathe through her mouth several times just to allow the relief to register. He was an American marine, she realized thankfully. The man above her appeared confident, and she knew instinctively that she was now safe. *Safe.* His fingers around her upper arm seemed reassuring as he probed the jungle with his narrowed gaze. Amazed at the sudden change in him, Alex took in the grim line of his mouth, his slitted eyes and the way his harsh features tightened with frightening intensity. Alex understood the necessity of his concentration. For the last two hours, she'd been doing the same thing.

And then, when the American shifted his attention back to her, his eyes became warmer once more and, this time, filled with curiosity. He leaned very close to her ear, and again Alex felt a sense of security in his presence.

"My name's Jim McKenzie, gal. I'm a recon marine. What's your name?"

A croak came out. She swallowed. "...Alex...Alex Vance."

He nodded. "Hell of a way to meet, Alex Vance. Now, I don't want you to talk anymore. Not yet. We're in heavy VC country, you understand?"

She nodded once.

"Good," Jim rasped. As he prepared to go on, he inhaled the subtle fragrance of her perfume, and the scent dizzied him, reminding him of a gentler, saner time in his life. He fought to ignore the sensations the fragrance evoked. "I'm gonna truss up that shoulder of yours so we can get outta this place in one piece," he told her. "Whatever happens, don't yell, don't scream. Understand?"

Again, Alex nodded.

She saw him smile, but it didn't reach his eyes—it was just a faint twist of his lips. As he rose from his crouched position, Alex saw pain reflected in his face and eyes. And then, as he straightened up, Alex realized in shock that his left leg, from the ankle to his knee, was in a makeshift splint. Four roughly carved sticks of wood encased his lower leg, wrapped tightly into place with vine. What *was* a recon? What was he doing out here alone? Alex stopped herself from asking. She saw him dig into an olive green pouch he carried on a webbed cartridge belt around his waist. He drew out a dressing, and as quietly as possible, stripped the brown waxen paper from around it.

Jim returned his attention to Alex, who lay watching him with huge gray eyes. He had to give her credit—she had common sense. She was doing exactly as he asked. Her eyes grew cloudy with pain as he gently pulled the flight suit aside and moved the fabric of her bloody blouse to expose the wound. Leaning down, he whispered against her ear, "Now, this is gonna hurt like hell. I gotta place this compress against your wound and make a sling for your arm." He reached across her, sought and found a small twig. "Here," he said, "put this between your teeth. Whatever you do, Alex, don't scream, or the VC will find us."

A fine tremble worked through Alex as she clenched the stick between her teeth. She saw the apology in his lean, hard face. Shutting her eyes tightly, Alex tried to prepare herself for the dressing to be placed over her wound.

It was impossible. As gentle as Jim tried to be, pain reared up through her, and Alex grunted. She bit down hard on the wood, the taste of it almost spicy in her mouth. Saliva dripped from the corners of her mouth. Her back arched and her heels pushed into the soft soil, her nostrils flared wide. Agony sliced through her shoulder like scalpels. Fighting back a scream that begged to be released, Alex dug the fingers of her right hand deeply into the damp leaves and soil. All her focus was on the wood between her teeth.

"Good, good," Jim praised raggedly. He saw sweat pop out across her furrowed brow, and saw her nostrils dilate. "I'm done. Relax...." Gently removing the piece of wood from between her teeth, he smiled as she barely opened her eyes. "The worst's over, gal. Just hang loose and I'll get you trussed up like a Christmas goose to give that arm of yours some support.''

The pain was nearly unbearable, but through the nightmare minutes that followed, Alex was struck by how humane the marine was with her. He was tall and rangy, and as her vision cleared, Alex got a better look at him. A couple of weeks' growth of beard shadowed his craggy features. His fingers were long and large-knuckled, and despite their size he was incredibly gentle while he made a sling of vines for her arm. But there was a coiled tension about him, as if he could explode in any direction. His alertness reminded her of a jungle cat's, and he seemed attuned to the most minor change of sound and activity around them. Occasionally he would freeze, listen, then continue to work on her arm. They exchanged no more words—only looks—but he could communicate powerfully with those cobalt eyes. Alex was amazed, as if some unexplained telepathy existed between them. She saw his eyes change to a light blue color as he knotted off the last of the vine behind her neck.

He helped her sit up. Dizziness assailed her, and she started to fall sideways. If not for the quick intervention of his arm around her shoulders, Alex would have fallen. Everything was happening so quickly, so efficiently. She wanted to ask him so many questions. Why was his leg in that primitive cast? Nothing was making sense except that he seemed to know exactly how to help her. The sling had eased the pain in her shoulder a great deal. Alex slumped wearily against the marine, her face pressed into the folds of his damp green shirt.

Giving her a quick squeeze of reassurance, Jim eased Alex upright. The look in her dazed gray eyes told him she wasn't doing well at all. Her face was waxen and perspiring, indicating she'd suffered heavy loss of blood from her wound.

"Gal, as much as I wish I could, I can't carry you," Jim whispered. Without thinking, he reached out and pushed several strands of hair from her dirt-smudged cheek. "You gotta walk. Understand? We gotta get out of here." He glanced up at the triple canopy overhead. "Before it gets dark."

Alex nodded her understanding. Jim rose, his hands on her shoulders to steady her. With all her strength, Alex pushed upright onto her feet. If not for his lean, powerful body as a support, she would have crumpled. His arm went around her waist, and she sighed raggedly in relief.

Without a sound, Jim felt Alex lean against him, and he slowly turned her around. Pain shot up his leg. The bones had been set only recently, and he knew that if Alex couldn't walk on her own, he'd have to leave her. When she weakly placed her right arm around his waist, her head against his shoulder, he smiled to himself. She wasn't a quitter, and that made him want to save her all the more.

The slow, torturous walk began. Alex was aware of the marine limping badly on his left leg, the side she was on. As she struggled forward, black dots would dance in front of her eyes. When they did, she would grab at his waist for fear of fainting. Each time, his arm tightened around her and he stopped, waiting patiently. When Alex nodded that the faintness had passed, he slowly began their walk again. She lost track of time as darkness gradually fell over the jungle. No matter how bad she felt physically, Alex felt safe. Whoever this marine was, he was confident, and that gave her the courage to go on.

The jungle had darkened to near blackness when finally Alex felt Jim draw to a halt. His lips scant inches from her ear, he whispered, "We're home, gal."

Relief shattered through Alex, and she felt her knees buckling beneath her. The blackness that had been threatening to engulf her finally did, and Alex heard herself moan softly as she connected with the ground. It was the last thing she remembered.

Chapter Two

Alex awoke slowly, moving through a constant barrier of pain radiating from her wound. She struggled to adjust her eyes to the gloom. At least her nose was working. Wherever she was lying had the dank, stale odor of earth. Slivers of moonlight tremored from some unknown source above her. Slowly she began to see outlines.

Jim McKenzie slept with his chin against his chest opposite her, propped against an earthen wall. Alex heard frogs and crickets in the distance. She appeared to be in a cave of some sort, the bare outline of walls rising around them. The ground under her was hard and unforgiving, but Alex realized that a blanket had been placed beneath her against the dampness. The flight suit she'd worn had been removed, as had her blouse. In its place, a thin blanket covered her. Carefully touching her dressed shoulder wound, Alex realized that her left bra strap had been cut away, but she still wore the remainder of the bra.

Her gaze returned to McKenzie. He was barefoot! Calluses covered the balls and heels of his feet. Her gaze drifted upward, and she drank in the sight of him in his rumpled olive uniform. Even in sleep, his hand rested over the butt of a sheathed knife fastened around his waist.

To the left of him she saw a few meager supplies, but couldn't make out exactly what they were. When she moved slightly, the marine snapped awake. In the same motion, he jerked the long, lethal-looking knife from its sheath. Gasping, Alex froze.

Jim had gone instantly from a sitting position to a kneeling one, knife ready. Sleep was torn from him. When he realized it was Alex who had moved, his shoulders slumped in relief. The terror in her huge gray eyes made him quickly resheathe his Ka-bar knife. He moved over to her, crouching under the five-foot roof of the tunnel—too low for him to stand upright.

"How you doing?" he asked, his voice shaky with adrenaline.

Alex closed her eyes and touched her pounding heart. "Okay. You scared me to death when you jumped like that."

Jim sat down, his right leg tucked beneath his body, his splinted leg stretched out before him. In the moonlight he could see the tension in Alex's face. She was in obvious pain.

"Sorry," he muttered, "it's a habit."

Relaxing as he lightly touched her left arm, Alex nodded. "That's okay." She licked her dry lips. "You're Jim McKenzie."

He nodded. "I didn't think you'd remember. You were pretty out of it when I found you. We're in a caved-in tunnel the enemy used to own." He pointed upward. "There's a small, concealed hole up there for air ventilation and light, but if we talk too loud, a passing VC might overhear us. Understand?"

"Y-yes." Alex watched as he leaned over and retrieved a chipped wooden bowl that contained water and a small piece of cloth.

Jim squeezed out of the dark green cloth, a portion of the towel he'd once worn around his neck to wipe sweat from his eyes. During the last month the towel had gradually been torn into pieces, serving many utilitarian purposes.

"I feel a lot better now than I did when you first found me." Alex met and held his warm gaze. "Thanks for saving my life."

His mouth quirked into something resembling a smile. "I'm glad I decided to go and check out the crash. I sure didn't expect to find a woman."

Alex relaxed as he gently wiped her face and neck, the water feeling heavenly against her hot skin. "Believe me, I never expected to be in Vietnam, much less get shot down." She lifted her right hand toward him. "I'm Alex Vance…Alexandra, but my friends call me Alex."

The shadows were deep, and Jim could see the terror banked in her eyes. She was trying to be brave, and that touched him. He gripped her hand gently and squeezed it. "Alexandra's a real purty name. You can call me Jim, McKenzie or Mac. Any of them suit." Releasing her hand, he rinsed the cloth in the bowl of water and squeezed it out again. "What *are* you doin' in Nam?"

Licking her chapped lips, Alex tried to smile but failed. "I was taking a helicopter from Marble Mountain to Firebase Lily when we got hit by enemy groundfire," she said softly. She closed her eyes, her voice growing scratchy. "The other marines, they didn't make it, Mr. McKenzie. They're dead."

He continued to bathe her face free of the crusty dirt and blood. "I'm no officer, just an enlisted recon marine. No need for any formality." He sighed. "I'm sorry to hear about those men dyin'. You're lucky to be alive."

Alex tried to hold back tears. Her gaze clung to his harsh, tense features. Under any other circumstance, she would have thought Jim to be made of granite, his face not handsome at all. But the way he pursed his mouth, as if to hold back his own barrage of feelings, told her he was a man with a conscience, and that made her feel better.

"You're a corporal in the marines?"

"Recon marines," Jim corrected. He cradled her right arm as he began to cleanse it. She had any number of scratches that could eventually fester and become infected if he didn't wash them clean. Picking up a small bar of soap, he scrubbed the dirt from her skin.

"I'm sorry... I don't know what recons are."

"You're a civilian, then? I thought you might be in the service."

"No, I would never be in the military, believe me."

The emotion behind her statement caught him off guard. "Not many women join," he agreed. "Let me tell you about recons. We're the elite arm of the corps. We get dropped behind enemy lines in teams of six men to gather information from the VC. Then, if everything goes well, we're picked up at a prearranged spot and returned behind our lines."

"I'm not too up on the military," Alex said. "I never knew recons existed."

"That's okay." His mouth quirked again. "When I didn't find any dog tags or identification on you, I thought you might be a spook."

"Spook?"

"Yeah, you know—a CIA operative. A spy."

Alex languished beneath his care. She managed a slight smile. "I'm twenty-two years old and a nursing student in Virginia. I graduate this coming September."

"A nurse. That's good," he said, washing out the cloth. Dumping the dirty water into a small stream at the other side of the tunnel, Jim scooped up another bowl of fresh and brought it back to where she lay.

He wiped her throat and across her delicate collarbone. Once he'd dragged Alex into his tunnel and concealed the entrance with brush, Jim had done the best he could to tend her wound in the dark before catching some sleep himself. What he'd seen when he'd removed her blouse hadn't been encouraging. "Then you realize you've got a piece of shrapnel sticking out of your left shoulder," he said now. He saw her eyes widen. "I took off your flight suit and blouse—" he gestured toward the rear wall "—washed both of 'em out the best I could and hung them up on those sticks wedged into the wall over there. It'll probably take a day or two for them to dry in this humidity, though."

Jim hesitated fractionally before pulling the blanket away from her shoulder to check the wound. They were strangers, and yet he'd nearly undressed Alex in order to tend her injury. As young as she was, Jim knew she must feel awkward at the unexpected intimacy of their situation. But he had no choice. He drew the blanket down to her waist.

Alex was too sick and worried to be embarrassed, but still she felt shy about her partial state of nudity. "If it wasn't for you, I'd be dead right now," she whispered, suddenly emotional.

"You're a fighter, so my money's on you to pull through," Jim offered. When he saw her cheeks flush with sudden embarrassment, he murmured, "Sorry I had to undress you." And then he managed a slight smile. "I don't make a habit of undressing ladies without their permission."

His quiet words dissolved Alex's humiliation. "It wasn't your fault." Alex twisted her head enough to look at the compress over her wound. "You saw the shrapnel?"

"Yeah. It's a pretty big dog-ugly piece."

She grimaced at his colorful description. "Were you able to clean the wound out?" she asked as she lay back, exhausted.

"The best I could. You fainted as we reached the tunnel, so I took advantage of the situation. I used soap and water to clean it out before I dressed it."

"Is it still bleeding?"

Jim shook his head. "No, it's swollen and bruised-looking, but there's no more bleeding."

Relief shattered through Alex. "Good. Is there any redness around the wound? Any red streaks?" she asked, thinking of infection or blood poisoning.

"None so far." Jim glanced at his watch's luminous dial. "You've been asleep all night. That's good." He gazed upward toward the source of meager light. "It's almost dawn."

Alex stayed quiet a long time, thinking. "How near is the closest marine firebase?" she asked finally.

Jim set the bowl and cloth aside. He wrapped his arm around his drawn-up knee while keeping his other leg extended. "About ten miles, if memory serves me correctly."

"We've got to get out of here," Alex said, her voice quavering. "I've got enough nursing knowledge under my belt to know that if I don't get this piece of shrapnel removed fast, I'll be in real trouble."

McKenzie heard the fear in her voice. Even in the waning moonlight gradually being replaced by dawn, Alexandra Vance was beautiful. The way her full lips moved, the fear in her eyes, touched him as nothing else had since that horrifying incident—Jim savagely shut down his thoughts, not wanting to relive that tragic day. Taking a deep breath, he whispered, "Alex, we aren't going anywhere. We can't."

Her eyes rounded. "Why not?" she demanded, her voice going off-key.

Jim pointed to his leg. "I busted up my left leg three weeks ago. My recon team was hattin' out for our prearranged pickup point when the VC discovered our presence. We were runnin' hard, and I told my lieutenant, Matt Breckenridge, that I'd hang to the rear to protect the group. I got pretty far behind, and I wasn't watching where I was going as closely as I should've been." He grimaced. "I fell into this underground tunnel. It knocked me out. The next thing I knew, I woke up five hours later in the bottom of this place, my leg busted up, and alone."

"My God. Didn't your friends come back to get you?"

Jim shrugged. "Normally, no marine leaves a buddy in the field, but I think the tunnel brush hid the hole after I'd fallen into it, and they couldn't find me. With the VC hot on their heels, they couldn't spend the time to look long for me, anyway."

"That happened three weeks ago?" Alex gasped, her gaze flying to his poorly splinted leg.

"Yeah. Recons are taught to be self-sufficient. I regained consciousness, realized I was in this place—" he raised his arm to encompass the space "—and started thinking about survival. This is an old, caved-in tunnel the VC used years ago, probably in the fifties, when they were fighting the French. That stream eventually weakened the dirt walls and the tunnel caved in. The VC haven't been in here for years, from what I can tell."

Alex could see more now that dawn light was cascading through the hole in the roof. The tunnel was about ten feet across and thirty feet long. At one end, loose dirt was evidence of the cave-in. She looked up.

"That ventilation hole doubles as an emergency exit," Jim offered. "Probably was a ladder there at one time, but they took it with them when they left. When you fainted, I lowered you down here as carefully as I could. I didn't want to start that shoulder of yours bleeding again if I could help it."

Alex met and held his exhausted blue gaze. The ceiling was about five feet high, and she began to understand and appreciate Jim's strength and vigilance. "You splinted your leg yourself?"

"Yes. There were plenty of sticks lying around on the floor. I had my knife, so I made these splints." Pride sounded in his voice.

With a shake of her head, Alex whispered, "Did you have any pain pills?"

He patted the webbed belt at his waist. "All recons carry a pretty good first-aid kit. I had some pain killers, and used a couple of them, but they made me too groggy. VC were all around the place. I had to keep a clear head."

"But...how did you eat that first week or two?" He wouldn't have been able to get far with a broken leg.

With a one-cornered grin, Jim said, "Well, now, I'm not sure you want to know."

"I do."

With a shrug, he said, "There were a number of banded kraits—poisonous snakes—that were makin' this place their home. That and rats..."

"Oh, dear..." Alex's stomach surged and nausea overwhelmed her. She shut her eyes, fighting the reaction.

"Sorry," Jim apologized. "Now, this past week, I can get around with the crutch I made, and I've mostly been living off edible roots topside. I found a VC camp nearby and stole some rice from them. Recons are taught to grub off the land in order to survive."

"Where are you from?" Alex asked, purposely changing the topic.

He grinned boyishly for the first time. "I'm from the Show Me state, Missouri." Pointing to his bare feet, he added, "I come from hill folk, and my ma and pa still live in a little cabin in a place known as Raven Holler. Ma makes quilts, and Pa, well...he makes ends meet by making white mule."

"White mule?"

Jim smiled fondly, thinking back to his family and the growing-up years he'd loved. "Ever heard of white lightnin'?"

"Corn liquor?"

"The same. Pa makes two-hundred proof in stills he's got hidden around the hills. So far, he's avoided the law. He sells all he can make. He's kinda well known for his white mule."

Alex smiled gently, seeing Jim's features relax in that moment. There was a burning flicker of hope in his eyes and a kind of dreaminess, as if he were back in Missouri.

"I like your Southern accent," she offered. His voice, the softness of his drawl, was in direct opposition to his rough-hewn features.

"And you've got a voice like a nightingale," Jim returned.

Alex smiled, feeling heat nettle her cheeks. "I wish I could sing like one. Thanks, anyway." For the first time since the crash, she felt hope thread through her. "I've never met anyone from Missouri."

"Outsiders call our people hillbillies, but—" Jim looked significantly around the tunnel "—everything I ever learned from my pa has helped keep me alive these past three weeks. None of those people who made fun of us or our lack of book learnin' would have survived this long."

Alex hurt for Jim. "People can be cruel," she whispered. Her father came to mind.

"What about your family?"

"I'm the only girl," Alex offered.

"Don't make it sound so bad."

She grimaced. "I've got two older brothers in the marines. My father is—well, he's a hawk," she explained, using the term that had recently become common for referring to those in favor of the war. "He believes wholeheartedly in this conflict."

McKenzie looked at her strangely. "And you? What do you believe about Nam?"

"You'll probably laugh at me, Jim, but I think it's all wrong. I don't believe we should be sending more and more troops over here. It just means that many more men who will get killed."

"Your pa's a hawk and you're a dove?"

"You might say that." Alex was suddenly thirsty. "May I have some of that water, please?"

"Sure." Jim reached down and placed his hands beneath her shoulders. "Let me help you sit up. You can't be feeling very strong right now."

Alex was grateful for his sensitivity. Biting back a groan, she sat up with his help. Jim took the handle-less wooden cup, badly chipped around the rim, and filled it with water. Alex drank thirstily. After several more cups, she felt sated. She wanted to remain sitting upright, and Jim released her. He located a rucksack along the wall and opened it. Producing another well-worn wooden bowl, he scooped some rice from a pocket in the canvas bag.

"I think you ought to eat," he said, offering her the bowl of rice. "It isn't much, but it could be worse. You'll have to use your fingers."

With a nod, Alex traded the cup for the small wooden bowl. The rice was gummy and tasteless, and she didn't feel like eating, but she knew she had to keep up her strength. Jim McKenzie's skin shone in the gloom, and she realized she was sweating constantly, too. The humidity was high and unrelenting in the tunnel, the air stale. When she'd eaten, Jim gave her a clean cloth to wipe her fingers and mouth.

Looking around, Alex asked in a small voice, "There aren't any more snakes, are there?"

"Not right now." Jim glanced up at the entrance. "Sometimes they fall into the tunnel." When he saw the terror in Alex's face, he added quickly, "But that doesn't happen often. The rats are gone, too."

Shivering and not sure if it was from her wound or the thought of sharing the tunnel with such creatures,

Alex said, "Somehow, we have to get to the fire-base."

"There's no safer place than right here," Jim warned her darkly. Sitting down, he untied the strong, slender vines that kept the splints in place around his leg. Each morning he checked the progress of his leg, reset the splints, which had a tendency to move on him, and retied them into place.

"But," Alex whispered desperately, "I *have* to get medical help, Jim!"

Jim's hands hovered over the knot he'd just tied in the vine. Grimly, he raised his head and met her large, luminous eyes. "We couldn't make that ten miles in the shape we're in, Alex."

"But . . . I'll die if I don't get surgery to remove this piece of shrapnel. We've got to try!"

Terror deluged Jim, and he crawled back to the tunnel wall opposite Alex. Adrenaline poured through his bloodstream, and his heart started slamming against his rib cage, his breathing turning ragged. Her cry of desperation triggered the entire terrifying sequence, and suddenly he was helplessly snared in the grip of the nightmare.

Alex watched Jim in confusion. His eyes had turned dull, as if he were no longer hearing or seeing her. Sweat popped out on his face. His nostrils flared, and as Alex continued to watch, his chest began to rise and fall as if with exertion. She didn't understand what was happening as he collapsed against the wall, caught in the throes of something beyond her comprehension. His eyes tightly shut, he brought his good knee up and buried his brow against it, wrapping both arms tightly around it. Minutes after his retreat into silence, he slowly began to relax.

"Jim?" Alex's voice was off-key. "What's wrong? What happened?"

Shakily, Jim released his bent leg and raised his head. He blinked his stinging eyes and tried to detach from the repulsive scene and its accompanying feelings. Alex's voice was soft—a healing balm. He clung to it, not hearing all her words, but honing in on the reassuring sound. Gradually, the scene he fought to forget began to dissolve. Wiping his mouth shakily with the back of his hand, he straightened. Finally, he forced open his eyes. Alex was staring at him in puzzlement.

"Look," he began in a rasp, "I can't *ever* go back, do you understand?"

"Back?"

"Yeah. I—I can't handle it anymore, Alex."

Completely confused, Alex held on to her own disintegrating patience. "You're not making sense, Jim. What are you talking about?"

He rubbed his sweaty face with trembling hands. "I joined the marines three years ago. Because of my hill background, they sent me to the recons for training and duty. I—I've been in Nam for almost two years—" He couldn't say the words; they jammed in the back of his throat. The black feelings, the grief and the profound sadness finally released him enough to whisper, "Recons are taught to kill a hundred different ways. I did—kill. The enemy. Men. VC who wanted to kill me." He raised his gaze to the earthen ceiling, his voice low and unsteady. "It always bothered me, even though they told me I was doing my duty. Killing bothered me.... Sure, it was the enemy and I knew it was often kill or be killed. But every time...every time, it got harder. I tried to remember the good that recons do, how we save hundreds, maybe thousands of other marines from dying with the information we retrieve from enemy sources, but I was hurtin'.

"This last recon patrol...it was hell. When I fell in this hole and busted up my leg, I knew it was all over. I thought I'd died. But then I woke up, and I knew I couldn't go back. I couldn't go to a marine firebase, recover and get sent back to the field." He shut his eyes tightly. "I just couldn't."

Alex sat a long time digesting his emotional confession. Jim had been trained to kill in a professional sense. She stared down at her hands and then over at his, clenched tightly into fists against his thighs. *A hundred different ways to kill.* Her mouth grew dry and she hung her head. "Then," she rasped, "you're deserting?"

Jim nodded. "Right now, I'm MIA, missing in action. They can't find my body, so they can't tell my ma and pa I'm dead. No one knows of my decision. I—I wish I could let them know...." He looked at her grimly. "If I take you to that firebase, they'll take me to Da Nang for recovery."

"But, Jim, if you could just get me close to the base, I could make it there on my own," Alex pleaded.

"You don't understand," he said heavily. "That firebase is ringed by VC. I couldn't just drop you nearby. You'd probably step on a land mine or get shot by VC before you even got close to safety. Even if you made it that far, one of the marines is liable to shoot you for not knowing the right password. No, you'd get killed, Alex."

Frustrated, Alex glared at him. "If I don't get out of here, I'm dead, too! So what's the difference?"

Jim winced at the anger in her voice. He couldn't blame her. Shame flowed through him. She deserved better than him—a better chance at surviving. Why had she been thrown into his arms? All he'd wanted was to continue to survive without being detected—by VC or friendly forces. "Look," he rasped, "I need time—"

"I don't have time!" Alex cried softly. "In a week, I could be dead! Is that what you want? Are you willing to throw my life away so you can stay safe?"

Jim couldn't bear the tears glimmering in Alex's haunted eyes. Anger mixed with his grief. "No, dammit, I don't want to let you die! But I *can't* go back. I can't!"

"Why not?"

Jim's breath came hard and fast, the pain in his chest so great it felt like a heart attack. He could see the anger flashing in Alex's eyes. Frustration showed in the set of her stubborn lips. "I can't talk about it," he whispered defensively.

"Can't or won't?" Alex hurled back hotly. She jerked the blanket aside, and the movement cost her dearly.

Jim's eyes narrowed. "What do you think you're doing?"

"I'm getting out of here, that's what. Get me my blouse and that flight suit! I don't care if they're wet or not!"

He stared at her, dumbfounded. "You won't be able to walk ten feet without falling on your nose."

Alex struggled to her knees. Pain throbbed through her shoulder and down her left arm. "Hand me my clothes. I'll be damned if I'm staying here with a deserter. I'm scared, McKenzie, but I'm not so scared I won't try! I don't know what Vietnam did to you, but I'm not paying for it!" She stretched out her hand. "Now give me my clothes!"

Glaring at her, Jim rasped, "You're going nowhere. Sit down, Alex. Right now."

Squaring off with him, Alex felt the pumping adrenaline suddenly leave her. She felt shaky, then began to tremble. Black dots danced in front of her eyes. She was going to faint if she didn't lie down immediately.

"You yellow-bellied coward," she cried hoarsely. "If I could, I'd leave you right now! Just as soon as I get strong enough, I'm getting out of here!" She fell back, the wall of the tunnel stopping her from completely collapsing. The jolt made her cry out, and she reached automatically for her wounded shoulder.

Instantly, Jim moved to her side. "Be still, Alex," he whispered tautly, pulling her hand from her shoulder.

Jerking away, Alex glared up at him. "Don't touch me," she snarled.

Chapter Three

Smarting beneath Alex's attack, Jim made her as comfortable as possible. When she lay down, he covered her with the blanket, then crawled over to the other wall of the tunnel. She had closed her eyes, her lips set in an angry line, and was refusing to talk to him.

Jim knew he'd better eat, even though he didn't feel like it. Glumly picking up the bowl, he dug into his rucksack for more of the poorly cooked rice. His stomach knotted. Only the sound of Alex's labored breathing filled the tunnel. How could he tell her the gruesome truth? What would she think of him when she knew the horror of the crime he'd committed? The crime was so heinous, so mind-blowing, that he felt as if he were drowning in guilt and shame.

Jim chewed the rice without really tasting it, his gaze fastened on Alex. Her breathing had steadied and softened. When she opened her eyes much later, Jim scrambled inwardly to lessen the tension strung between them. Casting around, he said, "In our part of the country, we don't have many television sets. My kinfolk—an uncle—had one, but he lived near town. I remember as a kid growin' up listening to the radio all the time." He forced a semblance of a smile, his voice low. "You remember the Lone Ranger?"

Alex turned her head and gazed at his shadowed features. There was something vulnerable and hurting about Jim McKenzie. But now his mouth, once a tortured, twisted line of some withheld pain known only to himself, had relaxed. He had a wonderful mouth, a kind mouth, and she had trouble imagining him killing anything, much less another human being. As he lifted his head to meet and hold her stare, Alex felt some of her anger dissolve. His large, intelligent eyes were not those of the killer he professed to be. She saw the faraway look in them and was lulled by his low voice. Wanting to make peace as she'd always tried to do in her own family, controlled by a father who ruled by anger, Alex responded. After all, Jim McKenzie had saved her life.

"Yes, I remember," she said softly. "I used to sit in front of our radio just waiting for the next weekly serial to come on."

Relief washed over Jim. He saw Alex struggle to be polite although anger still lurked in her eyes. "I can remember as a ten-year-old kid hardly being able to wait for the next Lone Ranger and Tonto story. I liked them, I liked what they did. They were always saving people who were in trouble." The corners of Jim's mouth lifted with the memory. "I used to make believe I was the Lone Ranger. I went out back, found a saplin' and cut it down. That was Silver, my horse. When I wasn't doing chores or huntin' with Pa, I'd be galloping around the hills, pretending I was saving people in trouble."

Alex shut her eyes. "I—I remember those times...the radio shows. That seems so long ago...."

"We were young 'uns."

"I was eight years old."

"Who was your favorite?"

Alex opened her eyes. "I always liked Tonto."

"He never said much, but then, he was an injun."

"I liked him because he saved the Lone Ranger when *he* got into trouble."

"I guess we both wanted to help people," Jim whispered. "Nurses definitely do that." He frowned. "I thought recons helped, too, but, I was wrong...."

"There's nothing wrong with helping others," Alex said. "You said recons saved a lot of marine lives. I think that's positive."

Jim smiled faintly at Alex. "Maybe." Her face held such serenity in that moment. She was pretty, and there was a wide streak of goodness in her, too. Desperate to get off the topic, Jim said, "You remind me of Molly Pritchard, a gal whose folks were our closest neighbors."

"Oh?"

"Yeah, Molly was kind of like Tonto, always quiet and something of a shadow. She had five older brothers, so she was kind of pushed aside in favor of them. She had hair like yours, the color of rich, brown earth. The kids at school made fun of her.''

''Why?''

With a shrug, Jim said, ''Molly was board-awful ugly. Not that it was her fault. She had buckteeth and she squinted all the time. A lot of city kids picked on her, but I used to stand up for her. Partly because she was hill folk like me. And partly... well, she was like a little brown mouse, so quiet and afraid. I always had a soft place in my heart for underdogs.... So, I kinda became her protector.''

''What happened to Molly?'' Alex was touched by Jim's admission.

''We were in the third grade together and this teacher, Missus Olgilvie, used to walk up and down the rows with a three-foot-long ruler in her hands. Anyone not studying got whacked across the shoulders. She always picked on the boys, not the girls, but poor Molly lived in dire fear of Missus Olgilvie smacking her. Molly couldn't see the blackboard, so the teacher kept moving her closer and closer to the front of the room. Finally, the teacher sent a note home to Molly's parents to get her eyes checked.''

Jim smiled fondly in remembrance. ''Little-brown-mouse Molly got her eyes checked at this fancy eye doctor's office. I remember the day her folks loaded everyone in their beat-up old Ford pickup and went off to the city. That was a big deal, you know? Hill people are real poor, even today, and we just didn't have that kind of money around. I remember Ma and Pa loaning Mr. Pritchard forty dollars of money they'd been saving, so that Molly could get this test and a pair of glasses.''

Jim tipped his head back and closed his eyes. ''The Pritchards came home late that evening, close to dark. They stopped at our cabin on the way home. I remember coming out and standing by the door. Molly was in her finest dress, a cotton print with yeller buttercups all over it. Her brown hair was tied up in a yeller ribbon, too. My mouth dropped open as I walked out to the pickup where she sat with her brothers. There she was, proudly wearing those black horn-rimmed frames. I stood there for a long moment realizing just how pretty Molly Pritchard really was, 'cause she no longer had to squint her eyes to see. No, she had the most beautiful green eyes I'd ever seen.''

Touched to the point of tears, Alex kept her gaze fixed on Jim's softened features. ''What happened after that?''

Jim chuckled. ''Molly went back to school wearing those glasses as proudly as I wore my marine uniform when I first got out of boot camp. The glasses gave her confidence, real confidence, and she no longer was a shadow. When Molly walked, she strutted, her head held high for the first time. She no longer had to sit in the front row to see the blackboard, and her grades started coming up. She turned from an ugly ducklin' into this purty young girl with huge green eyes. She wasn't a shy, backward, little brown mouse anymore.''

''I can relate,'' Alex whispered.

Jim nodded. "That's the reason you remind me of Molly—you're shy and quiet, but underneath, you've got real strength."

"I don't know about that. It's funny to hear you describe Molly, though, because in my family, I'm called 'mouse' by my brothers and father."

Frowning, Jim set the bowl of rice aside. "Your pa ought not to call you that."

"My father praises aggression, athletic ability and confidence. My brothers have those qualities—I don't."

Jim snorted. "Yet, you just survived a helicopter crash in enemy territory when no one else did. Does that sound like a mouse?"

Alex smiled halfheartedly and closed her eyes. His warm tone made her feel more emotionally stable. "You said you were proud to wear the marine uniform. What made you join up, Jim?"

He shook his head wearily. "Lookin' back on it, I must have been addled, but at the time, it felt like the right thing to do. My pa had been a marine during the big war, and all my life I'd been a weak, sickly child. I was tall and skinny, too.

"In school, when the city kids called me names, ganged up and pushed me around or wouldn't let me play sports with them, I would daydream, pretending the school was Dodge City, full of desperadoes, and that I was the Lone Ranger. It helped me get through school, I guess. One day, when I was in the eighth grade, these military recruiters came to our school auditorium and gave us a talk about joining the military as a way toward better education. I remember seeing that marine sergeant in his dress blues, how his uniform stood out from the rest, and how proud he was. His back was ramrod straight, his shoulders squared, and you just knew that he was a far better man than any of the others sitting on the stage, waiting their turn to talk to us.

"I went home and told my pa that when I was old enough, I was gonna join the Marine Corps." Jim's voice lowered with feeling. "I remember tears came to his eyes. Tears! I'd never seen my pa cry. He didn't say anything, he just grabbed me and held me so tight I couldn't breathe. When he finally released me, he took me into their bedroom to an old wooden trunk. I knew of the cedar trunk, but I'd been given strict instructions never to open it. So, when Pa opened it, I was in awe.

"There, inside, was his dress blue Marine Corps uniform, carefully folded in mothballs to stop the moths from eatin' holes into the fabric. I remember he took my hand and pressed it across all his ribbons and medals from World War II. His voice shook as he told me about each medal—the four purple hearts, the bronze star and the silver star. Pa was a genuine hero, and I'd never known it until that moment. When he'd finished telling me his story, he looked me straight in the eye and told me how proud he was of me wanting to be a marine like he'd been."

Taking a deep, unsteady breath, Jim whispered, "At that moment, I didn't want anything else in the world but to become a marine. I wanted Pa to always be proud of me that way. I worked real hard at school. I brought up my grades, and I tried to better myself. At graduation, Pa gave me a gift—his silver star medal. He told me to live up to it. When I joined the Marine Corps and put that uniform on for the first time, I *felt* like the Lone Ranger. I believed my drill instructors when they said marines were there to help the underdogs, to fight Communism and to free people. My folks came to Camp Lejune, North Carolina, for my graduation. They never traveled anywhere, but they came all the way from Missouri to see me. It was the proudest day of my life as I stood there at attention. My pa cried. He just threw his arms around me and cried.''

Tears stung Alex's eyes. "Wh-what did you do, Jim?"

He shook his head. "Marines don't cry. I just stood there, a head taller than him, feeling strong and good while I held him in my arms. I'd graduated at the head of my recon class, and I was given my private-first-class stripe right then and there. Pa was never prouder.''

Quiet reigned in the tunnel as Alex absorbed his story. In many ways Jim was like her: an outcast of sorts, someone who'd been viewed as a loser who didn't measure up in society's or, in her case, her family's eyes. "At least," Alex said, "you were noticed and praised for your efforts. I never was. My father named me after Alexander the Great. Can you believe that? He wanted three sons, not two sons and a daughter. Mom said he was really disappointed to find out I was a girl. He already had the name picked out, so they just put Alexandra on the birth certificate.''

Jim heard the pain in Alex's voice. "Any family would be proud to have you as their daughter. You've survived when most wouldn't."

"My father's probably raging and ranting right now that it's just like me to cause him a problem. I've always been a problem to him. He wanted me to finish nursing school and join the navy and I told him no. I know he's ashamed of me," Alex admitted, "because I've never lived up to what he wanted me to be."

"What did he want?"

"A tomboy, I guess. I liked dolls, playing house and learning to cook, but Father doesn't value those things. He wanted me to excel in math and sciences, but I loved painting and ceramics instead." Alex held Jim's softened gaze with her own. "I'm the mouse, remember? Father could brag about Case and Buck because they were football heroes. Both my brothers went on to get naval academy appointments and then became marines. Father's real proud of them."

"Well," Jim offered, "your pa is blind, then. You're a purty gal with a lot of common sense. There aren't many who would've kept their head after that crash, hiding and not getting captured. *I'm* proud of you, if that means anything."

Alex felt heat suffuse her neck and cheeks under Jim's praise. "I . . . thanks."

"You're shy. Worse than Molly Pritchard was at one time, I think," he teased.

"Mice are always shy," Alex muttered, refusing to look up at him.

With a smile, Jim added, "Well, in my book, any man would be proud to have you on his arm."

There was such an incredible gentleness about him, and Alex forced herself to meet his hooded stare. "Listen," she said urgently, "if I don't get this shrapnel out of my shoulder, I'm not going to live. At least dig it out for me, Jim. I can't do it on my own. If the foreign object isn't removed, it will create infection and blood poisoning." She looked around at the meager supplies positioned along the wall. "Can you do it? Will you?"

Jim's stomach knotted. Alex was right: if he didn't do something, she would worsen—could even die. And more than anything, he didn't want that to happen. "I wish," he rasped, "that none of this had happened, Alex. You don't deserve to be in this situation, to be stuck with me."

"It's a little late for regrets, isn't it?"

With a shake of his head, Jim slowly got to his hands and knees. "Yeah, it is. All I've got is my Kabar knife and a clean compress—plus soap and water." He glanced over at her. "I'm all thumbs when it comes to delicate work."

"I don't believe that," Alex said. She tried to sound confident and in charge. "Sterilize your knife the best you can. And get the compress, soap and water ready to use after you dig out the shrapnel." Her heart was pounding, and she was scared—scared of the pain she couldn't avoid. But there was no choice: if the shrapnel didn't come out, she was as good as dead. And suddenly, Alex didn't want to die. Surprised at the depth of her survival instinct, Alex found a startling determination flowing through her for the first time in her life. Maybe it was that backbone that Jim had talked about earlier. What did he see in her that she didn't see in herself?

"Okay, gal, I'll get the supplies together. You just lie there and try to relax."

"Yeah...sure. I'm scared to death, Jim. I'm afraid of the pain—of maybe bleeding to death once you take out the shrapnel...."

Leaning over, Jim pressed his hand to her good shoulder. "Hush, gal, you're gonna get through this just fine. I've got a good sense about it."

With a whisper, Alex said, "I'm glad you do. I'm just so scared—"

"Don't let the fear make you freeze, Alex, make it your friend. That's what I always do."

Alex tried to do as he counseled. She watched him light a small, oblong piece of metal, a magnesium tab. It flared to life, its white flame making the entire tunnel bright as daylight. A shiver of anticipation threaded through Alex as she watched Jim slowly and carefully pass the point of the evil-looking Ka-bar knife through the flame.

"If I remember my anatomy," Alex said, her voice strained, "there's an artery somewhere in the vicinity of the shrapnel. If it's cut, I'll bleed to death."

Jim looked up sharply. "I'll be careful." His heart twinged. Alex was too brave, too good, to die—especially at his hands. He'd already killed— Again Jim slammed the door shut on the haunting memory. Still, his hand shook in remembrance, and he released a long, unsteady breath.

"Just think that I'm Tonto, and you're the Lone Ranger come to help," Alex joked weakly, feeling sweat form on her brow and run down her temple.

"Right now, I wish I could be a doctor," Jim muttered. The knife point was sterilized. Jim picked up a small piece of wood. "Here, put this between your teeth like before."

With a nod, Alex took the wood. Her heartbeat rose to a furious rate, and she tensed. As Jim carefully removed the bandage and dressing, Alex shut her eyes and bit down hard on the wood. Oh, God, it was going to hurt. She tried to think of another time—when she'd broken her arm trying to emulate her two brothers by jumping from the roof of the house to a nearby oak limb. They had derided her, called her a mouse, a coward, until finally, out of hurt and anger, she'd jumped. It hadn't worked, and Alex had fallen twenty feet to the ground below.

Alex remembered screaming with the pain that had reared up her arm from the broken bone. Her mother had run out of the house to her rescue. Alex recalled sitting on the ground as a ten-year-old, holding her right arm, seeing her mother's distraught features. Her two brothers had gathered around her, frantic and unable to help. More than anything, Alex remembered her mother wrapping her arm in a towel. Then, when Alex had tried to stand, she'd fainted from the pain. If only she would faint from the pain this time. If only...

Jim sat tensely in the aftermath of digging the shrapnel from Alex's shoulder. She'd fainted seconds into the cruel procedure, and he was grateful for that. It had made his job easier. Still, there was no way he could shield his own raw emotions from the pain she'd endured so bravely. Looking at the fresh compress and bandage on her shoulder, Jim wondered if he'd done well enough. The wound looked nasty, red around the torn edges of her flesh. Gently, he touched Alex's slack features. Easing the wrinkles from her brow, Jim absorbed her quiet beauty into his heart. Even her lips were colorless.

"Little brown mouse," he murmured, and he continued to gently stroke her cap of sable hair as a mother might soothe a hurt and frightened child. Somehow he couldn't seem to distance himself from Alex, or the problems he saw ahead. She hadn't asked to be shot down, or to be here with him. The decision he'd made after— He shut his eyes and groaned. Well, at any rate, Alex was the innocent in this whole mess.

Jim knew his leg was healing, although he was in constant pain. But pain was something he'd learned to live with a long time ago. He looked down at Alex and knew his heart had no defenses against her. What could he do? He couldn't allow her to die. He certainly couldn't sentence her to the life he'd chosen to live. His hand rested on her blanketed right shoulder, and he shut his eyes. *What was he going to do?*

Alex groaned. The sound of her own voice pulled her out of her unconscious state. She felt a man's hand on her hair, stroking it slowly, and the sensation eased her pain momentarily.

"Alex?"

It was Jim's voice, low and next to her ear. She forced her eyes open to slits. He was leaning over her, his face shadowed, sweaty and tense. He placed his finger to her lips and she slowly realized she heard other noises . . . voices.

Jim gripped Alex's hand and looked up toward the tunnel's concealed opening. He recognized the voices as belonging to the VC who owned this territory. It was nearly dark, and they probably were aware of this abandoned tunnel. Alex had been unconscious, moaning off and on for an hour. He'd kept his hand over her mouth, fearing someone would hear them. Now, the VC were very close. Too close.

Sweat trickled down the sides of Alex's temples. She felt Jim's grip tighten on her hand. VC were nearby! Her already uneven heartbeat sped up with new terror. In Jim's hand was the Ka-bar. The dull ache in her shoulder seemed nothing compared to the fear surging through her. She saw the shadow of a man above the concealed entrance. Her breath lodged in her throat. Jim turned, tense and ready to meet any VC coming down the camouflaged access.

How long Alex lay dripping in her own fearful sweat, her heart thundering in her breast, she didn't know. The shadow disappeared. Gradually, the VC voices drifted off. Closing her eyes, Alex sank back against the hard ground. She felt Jim's reassuring squeeze on her hand, as if to reward her for remaining utterly silent. Opening her eyes, Alex stared up into his tense, harsh features. The changes that took place in him never ceased to amaze her. One moment, Jim was a country boy with a soft, Missouri drawl telling stories about his growing-up years, the next he was a tiger, ready to strike and kill without any sign of remorse. The change was frightening, but it also made Alex feel protected. She knew Jim would fight to save her life if the VC came down that tunnel entrance.

The danger was past—for now. Jim sat down and gave Alex his undivided attention. He took two pain pills from his first-aid kit and held them up for her to see.

"Take these," he rasped hoarsely, then slid his arms beneath her shoulders and lifted her upward.

Alex took the pills in her mouth. Grateful for the water, she swallowed them. As he laid her back down, she whispered, "Thank you...."

Awkwardly, Jim drew the blanket across her again. "How do you feel?"

"Like hell."

"Your eyes look better."

She nodded. "There's not as much pain in my shoulder now."

Jim held up the piece of twisted shrapnel. "If you were a marine, you'd get a purple heart for this."

Alex stared up at the piece of metal that had been lodged in her shoulder. "No wonder I fainted."

"Right after I started," Jim said. "I'm glad. It saved you a lot of suffering." He placed the shrapnel in her right hand. "A souvenir from the war."

She shook her head slowly from side to side. "What an awful reminder."

Jim couldn't argue. "Most of the wounds our guys carry around aren't the kind you can see, anyway."

"What do you mean?"

"My pa carried a lot of invisible wounds. I recall him screaming and waking us up at night years after the war. Ma said they were just bad dreams. But after Pa had one, he'd be in a dark mood for at least a week. Now," Jim admitted, "I understand why...."

Alex desperately wanted to know more about Jim, what had made him run, but the pills were already beginning to work. She began to feel light-headed, some of the pain receding from her shoulder. "My father was a navy pilot in World War II. I remember him telling me about some of his flights," she began, her voice slurring. "I never heard him scream or have nightmares."

"The air war's clean in comparison to being a grunt on the ground," Jim said. He wiped Alex's forehead and cheeks with a damp cloth. She was beginning to sweat heavily, and that bothered him. "Pa was on the ground, at Guadalcanal, Iwo Jima and other islands. He never spoke to us of those times, but I remember seeing the haunted look in his eyes." With a shake of his head, Jim added, "Don't look too closely at mine. I'm afraid they've seen worse than Pa's."

There was such anguish in Jim's eyes at that moment that Alex wanted to cry for him, for whatever terrible trauma he'd survived. "I—I'm sorry."

He smiled gently and bathed her neck. "You have nothing to be sorry for, gal. You're innocent." He added painfully, "It's always the innocent women and children who get caught in the crossfire of war...."

Alex wanted to pursue the utter sadness she saw in his eyes, but without warning, her eyelids closed and she felt a deep, spiraling sensation. On the edge of exhaustion and sleep, Alex dreamed of the Lone Ranger and Tonto riding together.

Chapter Four

Morning came slowly and with a lot of inner pain for Jim. Off and on through the night he'd tended Alex because she'd grown feverish. Afraid the VC might still be near, he hadn't dared to sleep. Instead, he'd lain on the ground next to her, his nearness seeming to quiet her. Sometimes he'd nodded off for half an hour or so before her restless sleep had jerked him awake again. Now, as the bare hint of light from dawn crawled into the darkened tunnel, Jim grew even more worried.

Alex was delirious, and when he lifted the compress to examine her wound, he saw how red and inflamed the flesh had become. Grimly, he bathed her face, neck and arms, trying to lower her temperature. She needed antibiotics, or she would die. And that couldn't happen. His mind worked over his limited options. Each time he looked down at her vulnerable features, a little more of his resolve to remain a deserter was chipped away. Yes, he'd made a decision to live in peace, to stop contributing to the war effort. But that decision hadn't included Alex. As he took in her glistening features, he could no longer deny his conscience: he had to get her help.

Alex's lashes fluttered and opened. Jim smiled uncertainly down into her dulled gray eyes. " 'Morning, gal. How you feelin'?"

"...Rotten...I'm so thirsty, Jim...."

"Figured as much. Hold on." He slipped his arm beneath her shoulders and gently brought her into a sitting position. He saw her lips set into a line as she struggled not to cry out. The movement of sitting upright, he was sure, hurt her shoulder, creating massive pain for her to manage. She lifted her hand to hold the wooden cup, but he continued to guide it to her lips, realizing how weak she'd become in the twelve hours since he'd removed the shrapnel. Thirstily, Alex drank three cups of the water.

As Jim laid her back down and pulled the blanket back over her, he said, "I've gotta get you some antibiotics. That wound of yours is infected."

Alex nodded slightly. "I feel light-headed, and I'm seeing crazy things."

"You're going in and out of delirium," Jim agreed as he pressed his hand to her forehead. She was burning up. He feared her fever was around a hundred and three, but he didn't tell her. No sense in alarming her. Her being a nurse put her in touch with those possibilities anyway.

Jim's hand steadied Alex's whirling, tilted world, and she forced a slight smile. "Last night...last night I dreamed crazy dreams."

"Like what, gal?" He took a cloth, wrung it out and placed it across her forehead.

"You were the Lone Ranger and I was Tonto. We were running from the VC together." Alex closed her eyes. "Isn't that stupid? I hate war, I hate guns, and there I was, right in the middle of it with you."

"Better to dream it than do it for real," Jim said in a low voice. When she opened her eyes, he smiled. "Did we outrun them?"

"Yes . . . but it was awful."

"Dreams, my ma once told me, are a good place to work out your feelings and fears." He gently touched her tangled hair. "I think that's what you were doing."

"Your mother sounds wonderful."

"A real practical lady," Jim agreed. "I miss her wisdom—I miss her cooking." He grinned. "I remember waking up mornings as a kid growin' up and smelling corn bread bakin', eggs fryin' and coffee brewin'. Hunger drove me out of my attic bunk, and I'd sit at the table with blue john, corn bread and eggs, eating as if there was no tomorrow."

"Blue john?"

He laughed softly. "Missouri slang, gal. Blue john is skim milk to you city folk."

When Jim smiled, the terrible tension in his features eased. Alex stared up wonderingly at his lean face. "Your whole face changes when you smile."

Jim looked away. Her compliment took him by surprise. "I'm just a lanky hill boy from Missouri, not a very good-looking sort."

"I think you have a wonderful face," Alex parried softly. "Your eyes tell me how you feel. And I like it when you smile...."

Jim refused to look at Alex. "If I were worth anything at all, I'd have gotten you back to the marine firebase by now."

"If you weren't worth anything, you'd have left me in that jungle to die or be captured."

Rubbing his face, Jim glanced down at Alex. "You carry the faith of the world in your large heart. You know that?"

"I'm an idealist," Alex agreed. "But then, so are you."

"Me?"

"Yes. My father's a congressman, and he's a realist. He's always accused me—"

"A congressman?" Jim turned toward her, astounded.

Blankly, Alex studied his suddenly tense face. "Didn't I tell you Father's a congressman?"

His mouth went dry. "No." His mind whirling, Jim knew without a doubt that all kinds of rescue missions would be sent to find Alex. It had been three days since the crash. Maybe that's why the VC activity around their tunnel had increased. The marines no doubt had sent in a recon team to try to locate Alex, or at least to investigate the crash sight.

"What's wrong, Jim?"

He shook his head. "Nothing's wrong." Every firebase in the vicinity would be on the lookout for Alex. Getting her safely through the net of VC to the marines might be possible after all!

First things first, Jim reminded himself grimly. "I need to get some antibiotics, Alex."

She watched as he moved to the other wall of the tunnel and retrieved his webbed belt with its numerous pouches and sheathed Ka-bar knife. "How?" Her voice sounded scratchy to her own ears, and she felt as if she were burning up.

"There's a VC camp about two miles away." He hooked the belt around his waist and settled his dark green utility cap on his head. "I've stolen from them before. I know where they keep drugs for their injured."

Her eyes widening, Alex whispered, "No! You could get killed, Jim!"

Surprised at her cry, he moved to her side. "Now, listen, gal, don't worry your purty head about me. I don't intend to get caught."

"But," Alex cried softly, tears forming and falling down her cheeks, "what if you are?"

He stroked her wet cheek, wiping away the tears. "Now, now," he soothed, "I'm not gonna get caught. Hush now, you just lie here and rest."

Reaching out, Alex gripped his hand and felt his strength, his gentleness, as his long fingers wrapped around her much-smaller hand. "I don't know what you did, but it doesn't matter," Alex whispered, her voice cracking. "You're worth saving, Jim McKenzie.

You're not a bad person, do you understand that? Whatever you're running from doesn't matter to me."

Jim smiled sadly down at Alex. "Gal, you're the kind of woman a man would be proud to keep company with. If you knew what I'd done...well, you'd tell me to leave." He gave her fingers a last squeeze and placed her hand on her blanketed stomach. "Don't get all het up over this, Alex. I need you to rest and gather your strength. Worrying about the likes of me is a worthless cause."

"No, it's not!" Alex felt vulnerable as never before. Perhaps it was the fever making her feel helpless. Jim's quiet and steadying presence had given her a fragile if illusory sense of safety. With him leaving, Alex felt a surge of panic.

The urge to lean over and explore her soft, trembling lower lip struck Jim full force. How clean, innocent and trusting she was. He felt dirty and guilty inside. He didn't deserve her. He patted her hand. "You'll be okay, gal." He slowly got to his feet, favoring his left leg. He motioned to his M-14 rifle lying on the ground, its wooden stock broken. "The rifle doesn't work. If VC come around, you're gonna have to be real quiet. Understand?"

Alex nodded.

"Good." In the semidarkness, Alex choked back a sob. As Jim limped to the tunnel entrance, she realized just how tall and lean he really was. There was a confidence that emanated from him, like a beacon of steady light in a heavy fog.

At the concealed hole, Jim halted. He turned and glanced at Alex's frightened features. The shadowy

gray of her eyes tore heavily at him. "If I'm not back
in four hours, gal, you wait until nightfall, then head
due north. That's where the firebase sits." He pointed
to indicate the direction. "Travel only at night, and
travel quiet."

Fear ripped through Alex. The horror of Jim possibly being killed or captured overwhelmed her.
"Please, don't do this, Jim. Not for me—"

"Hush," he whispered, and one corner of his
mouth lifted in the semblance of a smile. "You're
worth dying for, but I don't intend to let that happen.
I'll be back as soon as I can. I'll throw a pebble or two
into this hole so you know it's me coming back and
not a VC snooping around."

Before she could protest further, he lithely lifted
himself up and out of the hole. He covered the hole
with leaves and branches and was gone. Real fear ate
at Alex's disintegrating control. She wanted to scream
but didn't dare. Instead she lay quietly, trembling, as
fever alternated with chills in her pain-racked body.

Haunted, Alex closed her eyes and spiraled into a
nightmare world of the helicopter crash and the resulting fire. In the midst of the traumatic dreams, Jim
McKenzie was there, protecting her, taking care of her
when she felt helpless as never before. Her father appeared, yelling at her because she'd crashed and kept
him waiting. Interspersed were Jim's lean features, his
dark blue eyes twinkling with a smile, his face relaxed. Alex clung to that image of his face, to the in-
nate gentleness she saw in the curve of his mouth and
the way he'd touched her as he'd tried to bathe away
her fever. How could someone like him be a killer? It

didn't make sense . . . and then she capitulated to another round of nightmares involving the war that surrounded her.

Jim tossed several pebbles into the tunnel opening before moving forward on his belly. The sun was midway across the triple canopy, the light diffused. At the entrance, he froze and listened. No sound came from within the tunnel. For an instant, terror deluged Jim. He looked around to see if any of his camouflage cover had been disturbed. Dread had eaten at him all the way to and from the VC encampment. He kept picturing Alex being discovered by the enemy and dragged out of the tunnel. But the foliage appeared undisturbed. *Good.*

Easing himself into the entrance, his bare feet touching the hard-packed earth below, Jim quickly glanced around the tunnel's darkened recesses. Relief shattered through him. Alex lay asleep. *Thank God.* Quickly, he replaced the cover over the hole and sank to his hands and knees. First things first: he had to wash his hands before he touched her wound.

Alex awakened when she felt a hand on her shoulder. Her lashes flew open to see Jim crouched above her, a silent welcome dancing in his eyes.

"Jim!"

He managed a thin smile. "How you doin', gal?" He took the compress off her wound. The flesh was red and swollen.

"Did you run into any trouble?"

"Piece of cake." It was a lie, but Jim didn't want to worry Alex. He laid the compress aside and brought out an amber bottle. "Take a look—sulfa," he announced proudly, and unscrewed the cap. "Direct from Hanoi."

Closing her eyes, Alex whispered, "I'm just glad you made it back okay."

"I had the best reason in the world," he teased her. "I had you to come back to. Now, don't make a sound. I'm gonna pour some of this directly on the wound. I don't know how much it might hurt."

Alex steeled herself and refused to watch Jim. Surprisingly, there was little pain associated with the yellow powder he generously poured onto the festering flesh. He replaced the compress. There was something healing about Jim's touch, the way he cared for her.

"I had awful nightmares," Alex admitted. Jim sat next to her after retrieving a bowl of rice. He hungrily dipped into the contents.

"About the crash?"

"No, about losing you."

He shrugged his shoulders.

She watched him for a long moment and saw ruddiness steal into his cheeks. Warmth flooded Alex, and she sensed his terrible aloneness as never before. Over what? Too tired to pursue the topic, she asked, "Did any VC spot you?"

"No." Jim wiped his fingers on his pant leg. He pointed to the far wall. "I managed to steal us some more rice, too. I'll make it for us late this afternoon before dark. I don't want the light from the magnesium tab to give this place away to some sharp-eyed VC. Hungry?"

Alex shook her head. "Not really. Just worried to death."

Jim laughed softly, feeling suddenly lighter, better than he could recall in a long time. Getting to his knees, he brought the bowl to Alex. "I want you to try to eat. I know the fever's got you in its grip, but you've got to keep up your strength, gal."

The way he cajoled her made Alex respond despite how bad she felt. "You should have been a doctor," she muttered as he helped her sit up, then used his body as a support for her to lean against.

"You know, Ma said the same thing." He watched Alex pick up a small bit of rice with her fingers. "She said I was good with animals. I always had some critter around the cabin that I was getting well."

"I believe it. I'm feeling better just because you're back," Alex admitted. The rice was tasteless, but she ate for Jim.

Having Alex tucked beneath his arm, resting against him, sent a feeling of serenity through Jim. He sighed and closed his eyes. Her feminine scent, that special womanly fragrance, reminded him of a far less harsh world and sent dizziness tracing through him.

"You keeping company with anyone?" Jim barely realized he'd asked the question. He was afraid of the answer—and disgusted at the foolishness of his asking in the first place. How could anyone as pretty as Alex, and a congressman's daughter, not be attached to some lucky man?

"Keeping company?"

He blushed and cleared his throat. "Sorry, it's my Missouri slang getting in the way. Keeping company means going steady or being engaged to some fella."

With a muffled laugh, Alex shook her head. "Are you kidding me?" When she saw his suddenly intense gaze turn in her direction, Alex felt heat nettle her cheeks. Becoming serious, she said, "No. I used to have a boyfriend, but we parted ways a couple of months ago. What about you? The way you talk about Molly Pritchard, I thought you might be engaged or married to her."

It was his turn to laugh softly. "No, Molly went on to marry the captain of the football team—a city fella whose pa owns a furniture store. Molly did well by herself."

"You liked her, though."

"Yeah," he said wistfully, "I always had a crush on that little gal." And then Jim glanced down at Alex. "But I was this ganglin' boy who tried to go through high school barefoot, until the principal whacked me across the rear with a ruler for not followin' the rules. Molly didn't want to be embarrassed by the likes of me."

Her heart twinged with pain, Jim's pain. "I'd like you, shoes or no shoes."

With a chuckle, he glanced down at his dirt-stained bare feet. "You don't have much choice, gal."

Their laughter was soft, mingled. Alex glanced up and nearly drowned in the smoky blueness of Jim's eyes. The change in him was startling, wonderful. The urge to reach up, touch his unshaven cheek and kiss him, was overwhelming. Alex saw his eyes change and grow narrowed. Her breath snagged as she read that intent: he wanted to kiss her, too. The moment crystalized—then dissolved as the haunted expression returned to his face, conquering his need of her.

Returning her attention to the rice, Alex ate in silence. What terrible shadow loomed over Jim?

"What I don't understand," Jim said, trying to ease the sudden awkwardness between them, "is why you don't have a man."

"Mostly because of my schooling, Jim. I have a straight-A average—my father wouldn't settle for anything less." She gave him a wry look. "A congressman's daughter has to be the best at everything, didn't you know?"

He heard the sarcasm in her voice. "Has it always been like that for you? Those kinds of expectations and pressures?"

"Sure. Case and Buck got straight A's without ever cracking a book. Me? I have to study my head off night and day to make those grades. Mother says I have her genes. She struggled through school, too."

"This nursing, is it what you want to do?"

Alex nodded. "More than anything in the world. I'm a lot like my mother, I guess. She had dreams of being a nurse, too, but she married my father when she was eighteen, so she never got the chance. In some ways, I'm following her dream."

"I bet you'll make a fine nurse."

"If I can get past my reaction to blood," Alex said wryly. She finished the last of the rice and handed the bowl back to him. Jim helped her lie back down and tucked the blanket around her.

Busying himself with the heating tab and making more rice for them, Jim said, "A nurse who can't stand the sight of blood? What will you do about it?"

"There are lots of different kinds of nursing, Jim. One area that really intrigues me is psychology. I've chosen to go into psychiatric nursing."

"Oh, the shrinks," he teased.

"I know our society thinks psychology is for crazy people, but they're wrong. There are a lot of reasons why humans react the way they do to certain stresses, certain situations."

"No argument from me," he said as he held the canteen cup over the lighted magnesium tab to heat the water. The odor from the tab stung his nostrils, and he moved as far away as he could. It was a stringent, stinging odor. The smell of the magnesium could bring VC to the tunnel; it was a risk to do this.

"My ma said my pa was never the same after the big war."

"Battle fatigue," Alex guessed grimly. "Even now, I'm getting horrible nightmares that are a part of the symptom pattern. I'm sure I'll have them for a long time afterward. I learned those things in my psychology classes. I like understanding how our feelings run our mind and vice versa."

"Well," Jim whispered, "this war is going to do a lot of damage to every man and woman who gets trapped in it." Looking over at Alex, he added, "We're going to need people like you to help us heal afterward."

The question was on her lips to ask about Jim's trauma that continued to haunt his eyes and his voice.

Alex felt miraculously better. Was it because of the sulfa powder fighting her infection or because Jim had come back safely to her? Sleep snagged Alex, and she told him she was going to rest. This time her dreams were about Jim kissing her, and her kissing him back. The coming days would reveal her future. Would the sulfa drugs halt the infection enough so that she could make it to a marine firebase? Would Jim help her get close to one? Or would she have to try to brave it on her own? The questions were unanswerable, and Alex's torrid dreams turned dark and threatening.

"How many days has it been?" Alex asked as she leaned against the tunnel wall. Jim sat opposite her as they ate their daily ration of rice.

"Six." He pursed his lips. "Your wound's doing much better. I don't understand why the infection won't leave."

Alex felt much improved, with some of her old strength returning after the sulfa drugs had cut back the fever. "Probably debris still in the wound," she guessed. She continued to run a fever that would spike over a hundred every twelve hours or so. It was at those times, when she grew chilled and began to shiver, that Jim would hold her in his arms. For Alex it was when she felt safest—even happy.

A chill racked her, and she groaned.

Jim looked up and frowned. "The fever back again?"

Upset, Alex nodded and set the wooden bowl aside. She had counted on the sulfa drugs getting her stabilized enough to make it to the marine firebase.

Jim put her bowl away. Shadows showed beneath Alex's glorious gray eyes, and her cheekbones seemed to jut out from her increasingly gaunt face. Jim's conscience gnawed at him more with every passing hour. He had to get Alex to U.S. lines for medical assistance.

"Here," he offered, "I'll hold you till they stop."

Alex nodded and gripped the blanket, wishing mightily for a hot bath and a bed to rest upon instead of a dirt floor. But she kept her wishes to herself. Jim was doing the best he could under the circumstances. As he slid over and settled his back against the wall, Alex moved into the circle of his awaiting embrace. He drew the blanket up over her shoulders and gently placed his lanky arms around her.

"There," Jim sighed, "that's better." How he looked forward to these rare times with Alex in his arms. The last six days had worked a miracle of sorts upon him. Alex was a fighter, there was no doubt. She never whimpered or complained about the pain he knew she tolerated. When the VC were nearby, she huddled in his arms, face pressed against his damp shirt, trembling, but never uttering a word that might give them away. There weren't many with her kind of courage.

With a sigh, Alex relaxed completely in Jim's embrace. She pressed her cheek against his chest and closed her eyes, the beat of his heart reassuring beneath her ear. "I always feel safe with you," she uttered tiredly.

Jim whispered, "I feel whole with you in my arms, gal. Ma always said that when I found a woman who made me feel complete, I'd know how she felt about Pa.''

"I like what we have." Alex laughed slightly. "Despite the circumstances."

"Yeah, I sure never met anyone like you in the real world."

Alex nodded. "I'm sorry this happened, but I'm not sorry I met you," she admitted softly.

"No?" Jim smoothed down strands of her sable hair. Alex's face was waxen and glistening with sweat. He could feel her trembling, but she didn't complain.

"No."

It was his turn to laugh, only it was a strangled sound that came up his throat. "Gal, I'm a sorry lot in comparison to the men at your college."

Despite the racking chills, Alex drew away just enough to look up into his shadowed features. The day was waning, the dusk casting a grayish light through the tunnel. Raising her hand, she pressed it against his chest where his heart lay. Risking all the trust they'd built in the last week, Alex said, "Tell me what happened to you, Jim. What was so awful that you think you're the worst human being on earth?"

He looked down at her small hand resting against his chest. Her touch was wonderful, healing. "I—I can't, Alex . . . you'll think—"

"Hasn't the last week shown you something about me?" Alex demanded softly. "Please, trust me enough to tell me what happened to you."

The pleading quality of her voice sheared through him. Jim felt his heart mushroom with agony and guilt—and the overwhelming need to tell someone.

Slowly he lifted his chin to meet her beautiful dove-gray gaze. "I'm telling you," he rasped unsteadily, "you'll hate me when I'm done."

Adamantly, Alex shook her head. She gripped his shirtfront with her fingers. "Trust me, Jim."

Tipping his head back, he shut his eyes tightly and gripped the hand resting against his chest. "Sweet God in heaven," he said rawly. Jim cared what Alex thought of him. She was the woman of his dreams. And when he held her in his arms like this, he knew he was as close to heaven as he was ever going to get. Because he was surely destined for hell. His time with Alex was severely limited, he realized, hopelessness dashing his dreams. The stupid dreams of a boy, not a man, he decided sadly. He was falling deeply in love with Alex, but it could never be reciprocated. She was a congressman's daughter, a woman of letters already far more educated than he ever could be.

His mouth growing dry, he released a long, shuddering breath. "Okay, I'll tell you," he said heavily. And after he did, Alex would hate him as much as he hated himself.

Chapter Five

Jim didn't know where to begin. He could only gather Alex into his embrace and feel a trembling begin deep inside him. The taste in his mouth was bitter. Finally, he forced the words out.

"There's a village deep in VC territory that always hid us for a day or two when we came through that area. We'd made friends with the chief and his family. He had a granddaughter—about six years old— who took a shine to me. I always called her Kim, although that wasn't her real name. My uncle has a daughter that age. Her name is Kimberly, and we always called her Kim. Anyway, every time we came to the village, this little girl would single me out, climb into my arms, follow me around. When her ma would come to get her, Kim would start cryin' and want to stay with me. It was the darndest thing. She knew where I hid candy bars, and I'd pack extra for her every time we went on a mission in that area.

"We swung through the area on that last mission about a month ago. But when we got to the edge of the village, somethin' didn't feel right, so our team hung back." Jim shook his head and stared blankly at the tunnel wall opposite him. "It was just a feeling, an ugly feeling. Lieutenant Breckenridge sensed something was wrong—we all did, but none of us could put our finger on what it was. We remained hidden, and no one knew we were there.

"A couple of men we didn't recognize walked through the village during those hours. We caught sight of Kim and her mother. They looked unhappy, but they were going about their business at one of the cooking fires. I wondered if the strangers were VC." Jim shook his head. "None of us knew, but we'd been out on the mission for five days and we were hungry. We'd planned to stop at the village, pick up information the chief had promised us, eat and leave the next morning. One of our men—Stein, our radioman—had injured himself pretty badly, and Lieutenant Breckenridge wanted to get him some care. We knew we could get it at this friendly village.

"Finally, the lieutenant gave the signal for us to split up. He decided we'd stay hidden at the edge of the jungle and try to get the attention of some of the people we knew were on our side, to find out if it was safe to enter the village. It was a good plan. I got the job of trying to reach the chief." His arms tightened around Alex momentarily.

"Then, all hell broke loose. Stein was discovered by one of the strangers at the edge of the jungle. I knew they weren't friendly forces when they dragged him out into the center of the small village. The leader of these strangers, we found out later, was Binh Duc, the regional VC chief. He started shrieking to his men to gather the villagers. About fifty people were rounded up, and Duc took his AK-47 and started beating the old men, trying to get them to tell him about Stein, who was unconscious.

"I saw Duc pick up Kim, and that's when I lost it. I leaped out of the jungle and ran into the village. I yelled at the son of a bitch to let go of the little girl. The VC ducked behind the villagers, using them as shields. I couldn't risk a firefight until Lieutenant Breckenridge got into position on the other side of the village. Duc knew I wouldn't fire into a mass of people. When Duc turned, he smiled at me and put Kim down. Kim didn't know what was going on. She didn't realize Duc would kill her if the chief didn't tell the truth about us."

Jim shut his eyes, and his voice grew hoarse. "I saw the bastard take a black grenade from his belt. He knelt down, all the while keeping his eyes on me. I had my rifle raised, ready to kill any man who laid a hand on Kim. Duc knew that—" Jim's voice cracked.

Opening his eyes, his voice thick with emotion, he whispered, "Duc put the grenade in Kim's hands and crouched down next to her. I heard him tell her to take the grenade to me. She didn't know what it was. She had no idea it could kill both of us. I watched in horror as Duc pulled the pin, giving us only ten seconds before it would explode. On his command, Kim came running toward me, her hand outstretched with the grenade in it. She was smiling, thinking it was some kind of game....

"I—I screamed at her to throw it away, but she laughed and kept running toward me." He buried his face in Alex's hair. His arms tightened around her. "I—I didn't have a choice. I—oh, Lordy, if I had to do it all over again... I couldn't run, because Duc and his men had their rifles trained on me. They were all grinning. They knew they were using an innocent little girl to kill me... and they didn't care if she was killed, too.

"I remember standing there frozen, this horror washing through me. I saw the chief's face, I saw his disbelief at his granddaughter carrying that live grenade. No one could yell at Kim to throw it away, because Duc's men would have shot them on the spot. Duc wanted me. Duc used Kim...."

Alex raised her head, her eyes awash with tears. She felt Jim trembling and gripped his shirtfront. His face looked tortured, his eyes alive with grief, anger and desperation. Tears were running down his taut face. "My God," she breathed, "did you have to— Did you—"

"I shot her."

Silence fell in the tunnel. Alex sat up, her mouth dropping open. His words fell flat against her ears, and she stared at Jim in horror. He glanced down at her, then looked away as he wiped the tears savagely from his face.

"I killed Kim so that I could live," he rasped harshly. "My miserable life for hers. She was innocent." Then he covered his face with his hands and sobbed outright. "She was just a little tyke!" he cried, his voice strangled. "And I loved her! I really loved her. Yet I murdered her!"

With a cry, Alex lifted her good arm and slid it around Jim's hunched, shaking shoulders. He sat curled up, hurting. The sound of his sobs tore at her. She'd never heard a man cry, and this was worse than she ever could have imagined. She eased Jim against her small frame, his head buried next to hers. Tears blurred Alex's vision and her heart mushroomed with simultaneous grief and anger.

Finally Jim stopped sobbing and lay crouched next to her. Alex had lost track of time as she cried with him, cried for the terrible weight and pain he had borne since the incident. Instinctively, she knew it was the first time he'd admitted his atrocity out loud— probably the first time he'd cried for Kim or himself.

"What happened next?" Alex asked, sensing that talking about it would eventually help Jim.

He shrugged. "All hell broke loose. Lieutenant Breckenridge got the drop on Duc's men from another angle and our team killed five VC. Duc faded into the jungle. When the shooting started, I reacted automatically and took cover. Lieutenant Breckenridge found me later, and I was in shock. He knew it. He said he was sorry. All around us villagers were shrieking and crying. I was lying curled up on the ground—I remember getting up and finding Kim's ma. She was weeping and screaming. I—I tried to tell her I was sorry, but what could I say? Words were useless for what I was feeling, for how Kim's ma was feeling.

"The lieutenant said we had to get out of there. With Duc in the vicinity, we were only putting those brave people at further risk, so we left. I remember running late that night, with Duc's forces after us. That's when I fell into this tunnel and busted up my leg. When I woke up, I was real clear about one thing—I'd never fire a rifle again. I was done with killing. I had a lot of time alone to think, to feel. Kim was an innocent victim. I murdered her to save my own skin. And for what? I see her in my dreams. I relive it night after night. Why did I save myself? If I had it to do over again, I'd have run, I wouldn't have killed her. Better to be drilled by a VC bullet than to hurt Kim."

Alex shook her head and gripped his damp shirt. "No, listen to me, Jim. Kim was going to die anyway. Don't you realize that? I'm not an expert on grenades, but if the pin was pulled, that grenade was going to explode."

Jim forced himself to look at Alex. Her lovely gray eyes were shimmering with tears. How badly he wanted to take her into his arms, to hold her. Just her proximity took away some of the torturous agony he lived with. "That's not the point," he said, his voice gravelly. "I chose to pull the trigger and murder her."

"No!" Alex tensed, afraid her raised voice might alert VC to their hiding place. "No!" she cried again softly. "Kim was going to die, Jim. Who's to say you didn't give her a less painful death? A quicker one?

The grenade might have mutilated but not killed her. She could have lingered on the edge of death for days, limbs lost to the explosion. Haven't you looked at other possibilities?''

Morosely, he shook his head. "You don't understand, Alex—I shot Kim. I cold-bloodedly decided to take her life to save mine."

Her heart aching, Alex stared at him in the gloom. "Then you're really not a deserter or a coward," she said. "You let me think that."

Jim couldn't meet her eyes, afraid of seeing censure or revulsion over what he'd done. "I—I didn't have the guts to tell you the truth...."

With a small cry, Alex touched his grim face, feeling the prickles of his beard rough against her palm. "Jim, you did what you had to do to survive."

He glanced at her. "Would you have shot Kim?"

Wincing, Alex hung her head. "That's not a fair question. I refused to learn to shoot a rifle. I can't conceive of shooting anything."

Rubbing at his left leg, its dull ache always present, almost reassuring, Jim said, "I turned into a killer."

"You defended yourself the best you could under awful circumstances."

"I can't go back to the marines, Alex. I can't change what happened, but I can change the present—and my future," he muttered. "I decided not to take sides in this war. I'll scrounge off the land and be a shadow. I won't ever pick up a rifle to kill again. I'll die myself before I'll do that." He pointed to the M-14 with its broken stock. "I took my rifle and smashed it against a tree. I'll never use a rifle to kill again. All I have is my Ka-bar knife, and I'll use it only to help me get food. I won't ever raise a weapon in defense of myself again."

"That makes you a conscientious objector," Alex said gently, "not a deserter."

Miserably, Jim looked up at her. "Words... I thought life would be simple after I made my decision. But then, you dropped into my life." He kept picking at the vine knot on his makeshift splint. "At first, I was angry you'd come. Then, this past week, I changed my mind."

Shaken, Alex reached out and touched his slumped shoulder. "What do you mean, Jim?"

With a deep, ragged sigh, he shrugged. "You remind me of home, of my family—of things I'd forgotten about. So many memories, good memories, have come back to me while you've been here." A corner of his mouth curved, but his eyes were filled with sadness. "I realized what I'd become as a recon. I'd allowed my need for my pa to be proud of me to turn me into something I never wanted to be—a killer." He rubbed his head and hair distractedly. "I'm all screwed up, Alex. I'm messed up in the head. I got brainwashed, and I'm tryin' to straighten out how I'm thinking and seeing the world."

Alex sat quietly. She was grateful for her years at college, and for the psychology courses she'd taken thus far. If she'd ever doubted there was a place for therapy for victims of war trauma, she knew differently now. Aching for him, she said, "No one can judge what you did."

"I have to make that judgment. And I thought I had, but things have changed." He held her soft gray gaze. "I have to get you to that marine firebase, that's all there is to it. When I was sneaking into that VC camp, I realized you shouldn't have to pay for my screwups." He patted his leg. "I figure this leg will soon hold up well enough for a ten-mile trek to get you safely back to the marines. I know your pa's worried sick. He probably thinks you're dead. And I'm sure they sent out recon teams after the crash. They'll search the wreckage on that bird and find only four bodies, not five."

He gave her a sad smile. "I'll get you home, Alex, I promise."

Home. The word sounded so good. Too good to be true. Jim was mixed up, but his morals and values were still in place. Alex reached out, her fingers wrapping around his hand, which rested against his splinted leg. "I just want you to know that I know, in my heart, that you aren't a bad person. You never were, Jim."

"I'm a booby prize, gal, and don't you ever forget it. Stop looking at me like I'm some kind of special fella, 'cause I'm not. Just remember what I did, and why."

"In my eyes, you're a wonderful, kind man."

He shook his head. "Then you're a bit tetched in the head, Alexandra Vance."

Her smile wobbled. "That's fine by me. You forget I've been on the receiving end of your care. You're no villain, Jim. You never will be."

For the longest time, Jim stared at Alex. She was so soft yet so strong behind her trembling smile and damp gray eyes. "I don't know what it is about you," he grumbled, "but you make me feel clean inside again. Maybe it's you.... I don't know anything, anymore."

Alex smiled more broadly and gently touched several strands of dark hair dipping across Jim's pained brow. "Do you know what I want more than anything?"

"What?"

"I want you to come back with me."

He gave her a startled look. "No way."

"Why not?" Alex asked patiently.

"Because I've deserted. I'm AWOL."

"The recons think you're MIA, not AWOL."

"I won't pick up a rifle and kill again, Alex," Jim explained. "I'll refuse. And when I do that, they'll put me in the brig and throw the key away. Maybe you don't understand that marines hate deserters. There's no tolerance for them."

"You can tell them you're a conscientious objector. They can't throw you in jail for that."

He caressed her cheek. "My sweet, naive gal. You're acting like hill folk now, you know that? I didn't realize how dumb I was about the world until I got into the Marine Corps. Back in the hills of Missouri, we're isolated and protected. A lot of what goes on in this world, we don't hear, see or even know about. You don't understand the military mind, Alex. Deserters and conscientious objectors are seen as one and the same. No, if I turn myself in, they'll probably give me ten years hard labor busting rocks at Fort Leavenworth. I'd rather take my chances of surviving here in Nam than live in four closed walls. I'm a country boy, and I need fresh air and freedom of movement. I'd die in prison—I know it."

Alex said nothing. She had so much to digest, and her feelings were raw and sensitized toward Jim's plight. As she lay back down, she asked, "When do we leave for the marine firebase?"

"In a couple of days, with any luck," Jim answered. He tucked the blanket around Alex and gave her a long, searching look. Finally, he rasped, "How can you not hate me for what I did?"

She reached and gripped his hand. "Because you did it in self-defense, Jim. You're no more a killer than I am."

His mouth curved slightly. "You're bunny fluff," he teased in a strained voice, but relief flowed through him. More than anything, Jim had feared telling Alex the truth. It confounded him that she didn't hate him, that he couldn't see accusation or remorse in her eyes for what he'd done.

Exhausted by the marathon session, Alex closed her eyes. The grip of Jim's hand gave her strength, gave her continued hope. "I'm so glad I know you," she said, her voice trailing off into sleep.

How long Jim sat holding Alex's hand after she fell asleep, he didn't know. Her hand was so small and white against his own. He marveled at Alex's inherent beauty as she slept. Why didn't she hate him? Were his own emotions, his own horror over what he'd done, twisting everything so he didn't see correctly?

Stymied, Jim found no answers—just a lot of time on his hands to think about the sordid situation.

The earth shook. At first Alex thought it was in her nightmare—the jolting crash of the helicopter. But then she was dragged out of sleep to feel the ground beneath her tremble like a dog shaking off fleas. She gasped. It was dark. Blindly, she groped to find Jim. Her flailing hand was caught by his.

"Easy," Jim rasped, his voice thick with sleep. Dragging himself out of his prone position, he sat up and gathered Alex into his arms.

"My God, what is it?" she cried, clinging to him.

"B-52 strikes," he muttered. They were close. Damned close. Automatically, Jim placed them both against the wall and pressed Alex against him to protect her as much as possible.

"B-52's?" Her voice was high, off-key with terror. The ground bucked and shuddered in wavelike movements around them. Several chunks of rock and dirt fell from the ceiling to the floor of their tunnel.

Tarnation! "Yeah, they must be doin' some saturation bombing in this area. It's all VC-held, so it makes sense."

The ground groaned, and dirt sifted over them. Jim cursed softly.

"Come on," he urged, "we gotta get outta here before we're buried alive!"

Fear shot jaggedly through Alex as he hauled her to her feet. Dizzy, she gripped his arm as he led her toward the exit hole. More dirt avalanched down on them. The pounding and reverberation were increasing in intensity and power. Alex felt Jim's hands go around her waist.

"Climb through," he ordered in a rasp, and lifted her off her feet.

Blindly, Alex groped for the jungle floor with her right hand as she was pushed through the camouflaged entrance. Biting back a cry of pain, she struggled up and out of the hole. The brush scratched at her face, snagging strands of her hair. Her breath came in sobs as she got to her knees and crawled away from the opening so Jim could escape. Her eyes widening, Alex saw the sky light up with huge tentacles of fire. The shrieking whistle of the bombs carried through the darkness. The horizon lit up again and again, as one load of bombs after another exploded into the jungle.

"Alex!"

Jerking her head to the left, she saw Jim crawling toward her. "Here..."

"Man, they're gonna level this place! Come on, we gotta move!" Jim pulled Alex to her feet and placed his arm around her waist. She wasn't as strong as he wished, but they had no choice: it was either make a run for it or get blown to bits.

Gasping, Jim held Alex against him as they wove unsteadily through the jungle, the vines, huge leaves and brush slapping at them. He headed north, toward the marine firebase, their only hope of safety. In his hurry to leave the tunnel, Jim had left everything but his web belt behind. They had no food, no water. Luckily, he thought as they struggled through the jungle, the sulfa powder Alex needed to keep the infection down was in a pouch on the belt.

All Jim's focus centered on getting Alex to safety. She deserved a second chance at life. He knew he didn't. If he died reaching his objective for Alex, it would be an honorable end to his miserable existence. Every time she tripped, he was there to catch her. Only once in that first harrowing hour of constant bombing did Alex cry out. Jim knew how she must be feeling, but to his amazement, she seemed to draw on some unknown resource of incredible strength and endurance, somehow matching his demanding pace.

After an hour the B-52 raid diminished into silence. Jim breathed through his mouth, less noisy than breathing through his nose. He brought Alex to a halt and pulled her to him.

"It's over," he rasped near her ear. "At least, for now."

Shaking, Alex leaned heavily against him. "What do you mean? Is there more coming?"

"I don't know, gal. I don't know." He looked back at the jungle they'd come from. It was on fire, flames licking toward the dark night above. "One thing's for sure, the VC are lying low right now. It's a good time to travel."

Her mouth dry, Alex looked up. "Wh-where are we?"

Jim's teeth shone white against his glistening, shadowed skin. "Close to the firebase. I'm taking you home, gal, one way or another. It's just happening a little sooner than I expected, that's all."

"What about your leg?"

"Sore but usable. How about your shoulder?"

"The same," Alex whispered, clutching Jim's damp shirt. Her knees were like jelly, but she didn't want to tell him. Right now, he needed her courage, not her problems. The mosquitoes were thick, biting relentlessly, much worse than in the tunnel.

"Can you walk?"

"I can try."

"Good." His praise was husky, and he tucked her against him, his arm around her waist to support her. "No talking. If you hear anything odd, stop and point in the direction the noise came from."

"Okay." Blinking her stinging, smarting eyes, Alex put her full concentration into placing one foot in front of the other. Each step jolted her wound, and fresh pain jagged up her shoulder, into her neck and head. The night humidity was suffocating, the mosquitoes a constant nagging buzz. How Jim had survived in Vietnam for two years under conditions like this stymied Alex. Fresh admiration for him flowed through her.

Toward dawn, Jim called a final halt. Once an hour, they had rested for ten minutes or so. The jungle wasn't their friend, but it wasn't their enemy, either. Up north, Jim knew, in portions of the I Corps area, the jungle was so thick and matted with vines that it required a machete to chop through it. Here, it was easier traveling, and with his excellent night vision, they had made reasonable progress.

"Let's sit down," Jim whispered. He found a place beneath the gnarled, snaking roots of a huge rubber tree to hide from enemy eyes. In the grayish light, he saw how waxen Alex had become. Once she had crawled into his arms and laid her head wearily on his shoulder, he embraced her carefully.

"Is that wound bleeding?"

"N-no, I don't think so. How are you doing?"

He smiled tiredly and pressed a kiss to the top of her damp hair. "You really are a nurse. You're more concerned for me than yourself."

It felt so good to rest. Alex closed her eyes, her hand against his chest. "You're my eyes, ears and legs for this journey," she teased. "Why shouldn't I be concerned how you're doing?"

Jim laid his head against the smooth trunk of the tree. "You're right. I like your common sense, Alex. Just another good point about you, gal."

Alex warmed beneath his praise. As fatigued as she was, she wondered what Jim would do when they reached the marine firebase. Would he drop her off and disappear into the jungle? The thought shattered what was left of her courage. Automatically, her fingers tightened in the folds of his damp shirt.

"What's wrong?" Jim asked, stroking her hair.

"I—I'm scared."

"Makes two of us. You're in good company."

Just the trembling touch of his hand upon her hair soothed some of her inner torment. "I want us to live, Jim. Both of us..."

With a sigh, he leaned down and kissed her temple. "You're worth saving, Alex. I'm not."

Tears flooded into her eyes and blindly she turned her head. Sliding her hand around his neck, she brought him down to mold her mouth to his.

A startled groan began deep within Jim as her mouth, warm and seeking, met his. Instantly, the insanity of the world around them ceased to exist. Only Alex's questing mouth, her hand around his neck mattered. Inside, his heart exploded with such pain, such relief as he eased her lips apart and tasted her, that it struck him to his soul. Her breathing was ragged, her mouth demanding and wanting. Shaken by her need of him, he felt the walls he'd been hiding behind crumble beneath her heated exploration.

He framed Alex's face with his hands, tilted her head back and hungrily slid his mouth along hers. Fire, cleansing and good, flowed through him as he drowned in the splendor of her heat. Her mouth was like sweet, hot honey to be tasted, savored and absorbed. Jim felt like a thief, stealing life from her, but as the seconds melted together, some small functioning part of his spinning senses told him, right or wrong, she wanted this as much as he did.

The realization was as startling as it was heartbreakingly beautiful. Like a starved animal denied too much for too long, Jim took all Alex could give him. The pain he'd carried since that nightmarish day when Kim was killed dissolved under the caress of her hand on his face and neck, her lips sliding reverently against his mouth. For an instant, Jim felt hope. Hope. Gradually, as they parted, their brows resting against each other, their noses touching, he felt Alex tremble. So did he. This time, it wasn't out of fear, it was out of such an overwhelming desire for her that it robbed him of all thought except the feel of her in his arms.

Of their own accord, his hands moved from her hair, to her face, slender neck and shoulders.

"You're so beautiful, so good and kind," he rasped against her wet lips.

With a sob, Alex lifted her chin. Jim's eyes were narrowed with intensity, with desire. "I—I love you," she cried out softly.

Chapter Six

Jim's breath snagged. His arms tightened around Alex for just a moment. And then, he released her. They sat beneath the lattice-work of roots, with barely enough headroom for Jim. He closed his eyes.

"Gal, you can't love me. It's impossible."

Alex gulped but remained in the safety of his arms. How could she have fallen in love in a week's time? How? A portion of her was mystified by her blurted admission. As she felt through the morass of emotions bubbling within her, Alex knew it wasn't the wrong thing to say to Jim.

"I said it," she rasped, her voice cracking. "I meant it." Her fingers tightened on his shirt and she could feel his chest rising and falling quickly beneath her hand. Soon, it would be dawn. Jim didn't want to travel during the daylight hours, afraid of detection by roving bands of VC.

Groaning softly, Jim pulled Alex away just enough to look down and frantically search her gray eyes. What he saw in them was a luster, a wonderful trusting glow. He could never have imagined any woman looking at him like that—and meaning it. "You're feverish, Alex. You don't know what you're talking about."

"I've only got a grade fever, Jim McKenzie, and I'm not hallucinating! I know what I said."

Gripping her arm, he blurted in panic, "It's this crazy war, the situation, then." Such a huge part of him wanted her admission to be true. Hadn't he been dreaming of Alex in place of his normal fare of nightmares? Hadn't that small seed of hope that had flared to life deep within him entertained that very need— wishing Alex would love the likes of him, terrible faults and all?

Now, as he stared into her unwavering gaze, his mouth grew dry. He saw Alex's stubbornness, only this time it was in connection with her feelings—for him. "No," he rasped, "you can't mean it, Alex...you can't."

"I do!" Anger flared through Alex, despite her disheveled condition, the constant fever and the physical hardships she'd endured thus far. "You're *worth* loving, Jim. Don't you see that?"

Muttering a curse under his breath, Jim tucked Alex against him, losing the argument. Joy sheared through him, followed by utter hopelessness. "You love a loser, then," he told her harshly. "Don't hurt yourself because of me, Alex. As soon as I get you to that fire-base, I'm disappearin' back into the jungle. I don't dare get caught, or they'll shove me in the brig. I can't stand the thought of goin' to prison. I'd die in those four walls. Just let whatever you feel for me go. You hear?''

Alex shook her head. She was trembling from exertion, her legs aching from their forced march. ''How can I push something away that's grown so deep within me? I can't, Jim. Please, give yourself up. The marines don't know you decided what you did. You could go back and—''

''No!'' The word was ground out between his teeth. Jim placed his fingers beneath her chin and forced her to look up at him. ''Alex, if I went back, I'd go to prison for a long time. You can't go out in the bush with a marine squad and not carry your share of the load. I'm not going to lie to the corps about how I feel.''

Exhausted, Alex nodded. ''It doesn't change how I feel about you,'' she quavered.

''Go to sleep,'' he ordered tightly. ''You're stressed, Alex. It's natural to have crazy feelings at times like this. You don't love me. You just think you do. Now, go to sleep. We'll start moving again at dusk.''

Too weary to argue anymore, Alex nestled her head against his shoulder and closed her eyes. It occurred to her that loving Jim could be a one-way street. He'd never said he loved her. But that heated, hungry kiss had told her things he'd be too wary to admit to her. No, that one melting, soul-searching kiss had bonded them together. Forever.

* * *

Alex awoke with a start. At first she was disoriented, the dusk upon her. Then, as she grew more alert, she realized she was sleeping near the trunk of the rubber tree, alone. Jim was gone! Worried, she pushed up into a sitting position and looked around. Night sounds were picking up in volume as she tried to penetrate the lush jungle.

"Alex..."

A scream nearly leaped out of her mouth. Turning, she saw Jim quietly crawling back through the tangle of roots to where she sat.

"Where were you?" she demanded in a low, unsteady voice.

He grinned and held up some fruit. "Found some bananas for us to eat. They're a little green, but they'll be okay." Wiping the sweat off his face, he came and sat next to her. He gave her two of the small bananas, keeping one for himself.

"No, you take two," Alex protested. "You're larger than I am."

He grinned and handed the fruit back to her. "I already ate two I found."

"Oh."

Jim said nothing, but pleasure flowed through him at the wonder of Alex: she would share what she had, no matter how hungry she was. As they sat in silence, chewing on the unripe fruit, Jim frowned. Thus far, he hadn't found anything not to like about Alex. All through the hot, humid daylight, he'd slept restlessly, alert to any change in noise level. Each time he'd reassured himself that VC weren't nearby, he'd turned his attention back to Alex sleeping deeply in his arms, and to her unexpected admission.

Stealing a glance at her now—her hair mussed, her face scratched and smudged with dirt—a profusion of rainbow feelings rushed through Jim. She was so small and petite against his height and leanness as a man. Yet the soft set of her lips, of the petite chin that balanced her heart-shaped face, spoke eloquently of her courage. Alex was the kind of woman he'd dreamed of someday falling in love with—a woman ruled by a large, generous heart, who might look helpless but wasn't in the least. After all, the woman he dreamed of taking for a wife would have to be able to survive the harsh demands of Missouri hill life—not for the faint of heart.

"How's your shoulder?" he asked.

"Okay."

Jim smiled slightly and held her shadowed gray gaze. "Alex Vance, you're fibbing."

It was her turn to smile uncertainly. "Yes . . . well, it hurts. But so does your leg, I'm sure," she said, pointing to the splints.

"My level of pain is tolerable."

"So's mine."

"You must be feeling better. You're getting feisty on me."

Alex finished the second banana and wiped her fingers along her jeans. "My fever seems to be gone, at least for now. And I'm not feisty."

A grin worked its way across Jim's mouth. He felt such delight in discovering each new facet of Alex. How he ached to share each small discovery with her.

But he couldn't. The feelings he held for her could never be revealed. He had to protect her from himself, because there was no future for them. Ever. "Think we ought to put more sulfa powder on your wound? We're gonna be walking all night."

She nodded. "Yes."

Jim eased her to the ground and gently removed the bandage. He noticed that Alex shut her eyes and refused to watch him work over her wound. Taking out the amber bottle containing the antibiotic, he quickly sprinkled the yellow dust across the injury and wrapped it again.

Alex sat up with his help as he rebandaged the wound. The dusk had turned to bare twilight. "How are you going to be able to see?" she asked.

"Same way we did last night."

With a shake of her head, Alex muttered, "You've got the eyes of an owl, Jim McKenzie."

He smiled and gestured for her to follow him. "I've been called plenty of things in my life, but never an owl."

"What kinds of things?"

"Ladies don't need to hear those sorts of words. Come on, we've got a lot of ground to cover tonight."

Tonight was different, Alex decided quickly. They weren't being pursued by B-52 bombs dropping out of the night sky, and Jim was being much more careful. She was amazed at the way his bare feet caressed the damp, branch-strewn jungle floor, making no sound. Leaves swatted constantly at her face and body. Sometimes a vine would trip her. Jim merely tightened his grip around her waist, catching her before she fell and holding her until she nodded that she was ready to move forward again.

Hours later, they discovered a small stream. Jim carefully checked the area for trip wires and land mines before allowing Alex to go down to the bank to drink. They rested, hidden in the tall grass along the bank. Because of her sling, Alex couldn't wash her neck or arm as Jim could. He pulled off the olive green T-shirt he wore beneath his utility shirt and washed it in the stream, then wrung it out and moved over to where she sat.

"Want to get rid of some of that dirt?" he asked, his teeth white against his darkened skin.

Alex nodded. "Please," she murmured, grateful for his sensitivity to her needs. Jim positioned her near the water and wet her hair. Alex had never had her hair washed by a man, but she closed her eyes and languished in Jim's care. Taking the only dry piece of his green towel, he dried her hair. Alex managed to tame the damp strands into a semblance of order. As much as she wanted to talk, she knew it was impossible. Voices carried and could alert the VC.

"Okay," Jim whispered finally. He tied the damp T-shirt around his web belt. Reaching over, he gripped Alex's hand. "Ready?" They were making good time, and she seemed to grow strong as the night wore on. Jim was sure the sulfa powder was finally wreaking havoc on that stubborn infection in Alex's wound. She seemed to be regaining her former strength.

Near 0400, Jim heard a strange noise. Instantly, he pulled Alex next to him. His eyes narrowed as he scoped out the thinning jungle around them. At first, he thought he was seeing things, then he realized he wasn't. His heart began a hard, steady thump in his chest. His grip on Alex tightened. Straight ahead of them rose a small hill out of the jungle floor. It was the marine firebase! The hill was no more than a mile away, barely outlined by the first hint of dawn on the horizon.

Another sound, a more lethal one, had caught Jim's attention. No more than a hundred feet away, ten VC walked quickly toward the hill, armed and ready to fight. He felt Alex's hand tighten on his arm. She'd seen the enemy, too. Looking around, Jim spotted a mild depression in the earth. It was a crater made by mortar at an earlier date, he was sure. Worriedly, he gestured for Alex to move into the depression as soon as the VC column passed.

Alex tried to steady her breathing as Jim situated her in the freshly churned earth and began dragging banana leaves, blown off by earlier explosions, across her. She reached out and captured his hand.

"What are you doing?" she demanded softly.

Jim lay on his belly, his head next to hers. "The firebase," he gasped, "is about a mile away. VC are all around. They're gonna attack the marines." He held her widening eyes. "Stay here. I'm going for help. I'll thread the needle through the VC and alert the company commander to what's goin' down. I'll tell him you're out here. With VC all around, the marines will shoot first and ask questions later. We don't know the code for safe entrance, Alex. I've got to try to get through. I'm not risking your life, too. Stay put! No matter what happens, *don't move*. Understand?''

Jim could die in his attempt to alert the marines. Alex gripped his hand. And he was risking his freedom for her, too. "Why can't I go with you?"

He shook his head and released her hand. They didn't dare speak too much. "Too dangerous! I'll be back—I promise." A bittersweet feeling wound through Jim and he reached out and touched her flushed cheek. Sweet God, how he wanted to kiss her parted, ripe lips one last time. But that was merely chasing an impossible dream. And so was telling Alex that he'd fallen just as deeply in love with her as she had with him.

There was no more time to think about his feelings toward Alex. Jim withdrew his hand from the caress and backed away on his belly without making a sound. If he failed in this attempt, Alex could die. Everything he'd ever learned as a recon, the stealth and focus, locked into place. This was one mission he couldn't fail. He might never be able to atone for killing Kim, but he knew that if he could get Alex back to her people, he'd feel a little better about himself as a human being.

Alex pressed her hand against her lips, stifling a cry as Jim disappeared into the jungle. Up ahead, rising through the trees and brush, she could barely make out the hill in the darkness. Her heart pounding, she lay pressed against the mortar crater's wall, covered with long, floppy leaves. Jim could be discovered by VC. They'd kill him. He had no rifle with which to defend himself, only a knife. And even then, he wouldn't raise a weapon against them. He'd die. Tears leaked into her eyes, and Alex lay fighting back the urge to scream out her terror.

"Don't shoot!" Jim rasped as he crawled up to a listening post at the bottom of the hill. "American! I'm American!" He saw the two young marines leap to a standing position from their large, deeply dug hole. Their eyes bulged. Both M-14's swung into his face. Not daring to sit up or stand for fear the VC would see him, Jim put both hands up.

"I'm a recon marine!" he snapped. "Corporal Jim McKenzie. There's a VC attack imminent. Get on your radio and tell your company commander. I've also got a woman by the name of Alex Vance nearby. She's the congressman's daughter. I rescued her from that chopper that got shot down. Come on! Move!"

The youngest marine's mouth dropped open. It was the older marine, a nineteen-year-old private first class, who reached for the radio in the bottom of their foxhole. Jim nodded and slowly moved around so that he could watch the jungle front with them. Once the marine got the commanding officer, Captain Byron Johnson, on the radio, Jim gestured to speak to him.

"Hold on, sir," the marine said.

Jim nodded his thanks and took the radio. Quickly, he gave his name, rank and serial number. His eyes pinned on the jungle, he gave the officer all the vital information. His report was greeted with stunned silence.

"Get in here, Corporal McKenzie," the company commander ordered after a moment.

"Yes, sir." Jim handed back the radio and began crawling toward the line of concertina wire strung like three separate walls around the base of Hill 223. There was an opening through each of them, and once he passed the last wall of wire, he got up and sprinted the final two hundred feet as best he could on his splinted leg.

At the top of the hill a wide trench held several more marines, their M-14's locked and loaded. As Jim slid down into the trench, a gunny sergeant whose face looked like it had been kicked in by a boot, met him.

"Name's Gunny Whitman. Come with me, son. The CO wants to talk to you down in his command bunker." The gunny looked down at his leg. "What outfit you with?"

Jim gave his outfit designation.

The gunny grunted as they crouched and trotted down the trench toward a bunker, a large rectangular hole dug into the ground and surrounded with hundreds of sandbags. The roof was made of huge rubber-tree logs covered with more sandbags.

Captain Byron Johnson, a marine in his mid-twenties with a black crew cut and dark brown eyes, stoically listened to Jim's story. The gunny sat nearby, his grizzled features set in a scowl. When Jim finished, he looked at the marine officer directly.

"Sir, I want you to know I deserted," Jim said. "I was going to stay in the jungle and wait out this war. I'm not killing again. I'll go out and bring Miss Vance in if you give me cover fire. But I won't man a position, so there's no use in giving me a rifle." Jim saw the officer's face go purple with fury, his brown eyes hard with rage.

Gunny Whitman got up and placed his hand on the officer's tense shoulder. "Cap'n, before we assume anything about this corporal, let's call Da Nang, get ahold of Lieutenant Breckenridge and see if his story's true. In the meantime, I'll get the standby company ready for the VC attack, as well as get the arty net zeroed in."

"Very well," Johnson snapped. He glared at Jim and jabbed a finger at him. "You don't move a muscle, McKenzie."

"Yes, sir." Worriedly, Jim looked out of the deep underground bunker. He'd told the captain about possible VC attack. Alex was out there alone, unprotected and unable to defend herself. Looking up, he saw the gunny walk back to the radio operator at the rear of the stuffy, dimly lit bunker. Down another tunnel was the medical area, where those who had been wounded the previous day were waiting for a medevac to fly in and take them to safety.

After fifteen minutes that felt like a lifetime to Jim, the captain and gunny came back over to him. Johnson eyed him warily.

"I just talked to Lieutenant Breckenridge. He says you're MIA, not AWOL. Just what the hell's going on here, Corporal?"

"Look, I'll explain later, if you don't mind, Captain. We gotta get Miss Vance in here! Every minute puts her life on the line. She's wounded. You need a medevac for her. The VC look like they're massing for an attack at dawn. If—"

"The boy's right, sir," Gunny Whitman interrupted. "Let's get the woman in here and unravel this other thing with McKenzie later."

Johnson glared at Jim. "Who's to say you won't leave and never come back?"

"I'll come back, sir. You've got my word."

"Your word's no good!"

"Cap'n, with all due respect," Whitman pleaded in a growly tone, "let this recon do his duty, sir. He brought the woman this far. I trust him to bring her in. We're sitting on top of an imminent VC attack. Let's get her in here."

Relief plunged through Jim as the captain nodded. The gunny patted his shoulder and gave him the nod to leave. Just as Jim reached the top of the bunker, which led into the elaborate trench system dug around the hill, the first VC mortars whistled toward them.

"Incoming!" screamed a marine in the trench, and everyone flattened against the earth.

Cursing, Jim hugged the ground, his head buried beneath his hands. The mortar exploded down the hill, blowing away part of the concertina. Curses and shouts filled the air as Gunny Whitman went charging down the trench system to get the marines prepared for the VC assault.

Without looking back, Jim made his way out of the trench, and through the three concertina gates. More mortar shells were being walked up the hill, becoming more accurate with each hit. The VC were firing away from where Alex was hidden, and for that, Jim was grateful. He had no choice, he decided. If Alex remained where she was, she would be killed as soon as counteroffensive fire began. Or the retreating VC could spot her and take her prisoner. Moving quickly past the last listening post, Jim told the two frightened marines he'd return with a woman shortly and not to shoot. Both marines nodded, their faces strained and pale in the dawn light.

His heart pounding, Jim reached the jungle wall, got stiffly to his feet, then disappeared into the foliage. The adrenaline pouring through him made him hyperalert. Every sound seemed magnified a hundredfold. The odor of rice and fish alerted him that a VC soldier was very near. Behind him, he heard the marines opening up with rifle fire. More mortars began to fall and explode. The earth shook. The stinging smell of gunpowder hurt his flared nostrils as he hobbled toward Alex's hiding place.

Just as he reached Alex, marine artillery began exploding around him. With a curse, Jim jerked off the banana leaves. To his relief, Alex was curled up in a tight ball in the bottom of the crater.

"Come on!" he yelled above the din, thrusting out his hand to her.

Alex gripped Jim's hand and was hauled up out of the crater. Dirt, rocks and tree bark pelted them. Biting back a cry, Alex followed Jim, clinging to his hand. Bullets sang around her, crashing and ricocheting through the jungle. More than once Jim pulled her down beside him and protected her with his body. Each time, the artillery shell would explode, and Jim would pull her up and begin to run for the hill again.

Alex knew she was going to die. She could taste it in her mouth. The battle joined with new ferocity just as

Jim guided her out of the jungle and toward the listening post. They needn't have worried about the two frightened marines shooting at them. The LP was abandoned, the marines ordered to withdraw because all the territory outside the concertina wire was now considered enemy territory.

Bullets slammed into the earth nearby, geysers of dirt spewing into the air. Alex crawled through the concertina with Jim's help. More mortars exploded, Jim throwing himself across her to protect her each time. How many times he'd been hit by falling debris—or even shrapnel—Alex didn't know.

At the top of the hill Alex saw several marines put down their weapons, their hands reaching outward, grasping for her. With their help, Jim guided her into the trench. Alex's knees collapsed as she rolled into the safety of the trench. All around her she saw the frightened faces of young marines, staring at her as if she were an alien who had just dropped in from outer space.

"Get up!" Jim shouted, and he leaned over, gripping Alex by the waist and forcing her to her feet. "The bunker! Get to the command bunker!"

Dazed, Alex felt the steadying hands of other marines guiding her toward what looked like a darkened cave surrounded by sandbags. At the entrance, she felt Jim's arm go around her waist and guide her down the series of rough-hewn wooden steps. Her legs were so wobbly she was afraid she would fall. Suddenly they stopped and, blinking, out of breath, Alex looked up. They stood at the bottom of the steps. Naked light bulbs were strung along the dirt-and-sandbag walls. At least five marines there manned radios at one end. A navy corpsman, blond and baby-faced, ran past Alex, heading out of the bunker.

"Come on," Jim urged, his voice strained. He guided her toward another tunnel. "This medic's got things set up in here. Stay here, Alex," he said, guiding her to a wooden stool. "Stay here and don't move." At least four marines sat around her, all wounded.

"Jim!"

He turned back. Alex was frightened, her eyes huge with fear.

"I'm gonna get the corpsman, Alex. Just stay here. It's safer."

Gasping for breath, Alex sat shaking on the stool. She looked at the marines. They stared back at her in disbelief. Adrenaline was kicking in hard, and she shook badly. The bunker quivered from the near-misses of VC mortars. Alex heard shouts, screams and orders rising above the din of warfare. Shutting her eyes, she tried not to cry out, tried not to scream. Jim was gone. But where? Had he run away? Had he disappeared back into the jungle?

No! her heart cried. Lifting her chin, Alex saw a young navy corpsman carrying in a badly wounded marine. The man helping him was Jim McKenzie. Alex sobbed. Jim wasn't a coward, and she knew it. The unconscious marine was laid at her feet, and Alex got out of the way. Jim had turned and hobbled back into the trench. The corpsman quickly went to work.

Alex leaned over the medic. "Let me help. I'm a nurse."

He glanced up, relief etched in his eyes. "Great! Get me the scissors over there. And the dressings." He pointed to a dark green canvas bag against the wall. "Hurry! I'm losin' this guy. Hurry!"

Time blurred to a halt. Alex was aware of the mortar attack, the M-14's barking harshly against the enemy trying to overrun the hill. Jim came in time and again, carrying more wounded marines. Alex didn't have time to talk to him. She found herself on her knees helping Peters, the corpsman. As the battle waged and dawn crawled up the horizon, Alex found out from a marine with a leg wound that they were surrounded and heavily outnumbered.

"If they don't get air and arty in here, we're goners," the private whispered.

Alex turned to Peters. "Is he right?" Her voice was way off-key.

"Yes, ma'am," Peters replied calmly. "They've had us pinned down here for two weeks. We're low on ammo and supplies. The last medevac helo that tried to take out the wounded was grounded by bad weather."

"Then," Alex quavered, "we could all die."

Peters nodded and took the compress from her hand. "Yeah, but not without one hell of a fight."

Chapter Seven

Jim was worried but didn't say anything. His leg was bothering him, his limp pronounced. As he helped another wounded marine into the underground bunker for medical treatment, he saw Alex sitting down in the corner, her hand pressed against her eyes.

Delivering the marine to Peters, Jim walked between rows of men already in battle dressings, either lying down or sitting against the walls of the shuddering bunker as they waited stoically for a medevac. For the last hour, the battle had raged nonstop outside. Jim had delivered ammunition, helped relay messages to the front line when communications broke down and taken wounded out of the line of fire and to the safety of the bunker for medical attention.

Just as he was about to check on Alex, a runner gripped his arm.

"Captain Johnson wants to see you pronto," he gasped, breathing hard.

Nodding, Jim reluctantly turned away, heading out of the humid, dank tunnel and back into the main area of the huge underground bunker. Captain Johnson was hovering over the radio operators. Inwardly, Jim thought of his own skipper, Matt Breckenridge, who would have been up in the trenches with his men, not down here taking cover in a bunker. The men taking the heat topside were being held together by Gunny Whitman, who knew what personal leadership was all about. Johnson was one of those officers who cared more about his own skin than that of his men.

"Sir, you wanted to see me?"

Johnson's head snapped up. He jerked around. "You," he ground out. "I'm ordering you to pick up a rifle *right now* and get out in the trenches."

Jim's stomach knotted. One look into Johnson's narrowed, angry eyes, and he knew the captain wasn't going to take no for an answer. "Sir, with all due respect, I can't—won't—pick up a rifle."

Johnson's lips pulled away from his teeth as, livid, he repeated, "One last time, McKenzie. I'm ordering you to pick up a rifle and get your ass up there."

Out of the corner of his eye, Jim saw Gunny Whitman come barreling down the wooden steps into the bunker, his face set. "Sir, I'll help any other way I can—"

With a hiss, Johnson gripped Jim by the shirtfront. If not for Gunny Whitman's intervention, Jim would have been slammed against the wall of the bunker.

"Captain!" Whitman breathed as he gripped the officer's arm. "Calm down, sir."

"This bastard thinks he can disobey a direct order. He's got another think coming!" Johnson snarled, glaring into Jim's face.

Whitman gently loosened Johnson's hand on Jim's utilities. "Yes, sir, but we've got more important things to address. The VC are trying a rear assault. We've got to get arty called into position or we'll be overrun."

Johnson's eyes widened considerably. With a curse, he released Jim. "You're on report, McKenzie, for disobeying a direct order from a superior officer. You got that?"

Jim nodded. "Yes, sir."

Whitman glanced over at him. "Corporal, you're needed topside. We got wounded."

With a nod, Jim whispered, "Right away, Gunny. I'll go get 'em."

Whitman grabbed Jim's arm. "Son, be careful. They're exposed. You could get killed just tryin' to reach them."

"I'll be careful, Gunny." As he hurried up the steps, Jim worried more for Alex than himself. She didn't look good. He knew that if he was going to survive, he had to think clearly, despite his exhaustion. First, he had to get those wounded marines to safety. Then, if he had time, he'd visit Alex.

Alex felt Jim's nearness and opened her eyes. She managed a slight smile as he hunched down, his long, large-knuckled hands against his thighs.

"Are you okay?" she asked wearily.

He tipped his cap back on his head. "No sweat, gal." His eyes narrowed with worry. "You're looking peaked."

"I've been working a little too hard. I'm not as strong as I thought...."

He brushed several strands of hair away from her brow. "That's another thing I like about you," he whispered, his voice suddenly emotional. Despite Alex's disheveled appearance, she was beautiful. She needed to climb out of her filthy clothes, wash her hair and take a hot shower. But her gray eyes shone with such luster that he felt as if his heart were tumbling on the wings of pure joy. She loved him. Jim could feel it from her tender look alone. It left him humbled and in awe.

"Listen, we're getting the help we need to break that stalemate topside. The jets are gonna start dropping napalm any moment now, and we've got a bunch of medevacs coming for these grunts—and you."

Alex frowned. "What about you?"

He grinned tiredly and straightened. "Me? Marines don't hat out when they're tied down. I'll stay until it's over."

"What are you doing up there?"

"Mostly helping the wounded. Sometimes I trundle ammo to the grunts in the trench." He shrugged. "The gunny has me giving pep talks to some of the younger marines who are worried about being overrun. I sort of fill in the gaps where he needs me."

Alex was proud of Jim, proud of his commitment despite his vow never to pick up another rifle. "You're so special," Alex quavered.

Jim shook his head. "Gal, you must be plumb out of your head with fever again," he teased. With a wave of his hand, he turned. "Stay here and stay safe. When the medevacs land, we're going to get you out. The weather's finally lifting, and we can get them in here—providing the VC don't shoot them out of the sky."

Alex had never realized what it took for the heroic medevac pilots to land their aircraft under the withering hail of small-arms fire. The first one came in and the worst cases, marines who needed immediate surgery, were hustled on board by men who risked their lives just getting their buddies onto the helicopter. It was on the third helicopter that Jim personally took charge of including Alex with several of the less seriously wounded marines.

She didn't have time to say goodbye as he thrust her up onto the lip of the aircraft and the crew chief guided her to a nylon-covered seat at the rear.

"I'll make sure you get home...or at least as far as Da Nang," Jim promised with a shout, and lifted his hand before quickly moving off the crown of the hill where he was a target. Mortars still dropped sporadically around them, and the helicopters were perfect targets.

Alex opened her mouth to say goodbye, but the craft lifted off, straining with its full load of wounded. Despite the way her mind was shorting out with exhaustion, Alex wondered if and when Jim would get off that embattled hill. The last she'd heard, there was still the possibility of it being overrun. Fighting to hold together her shredded emotions, Alex bent her head so no one could see her tears. She was going to Da Nang, to safety. Never in her life had anything sounded so good—but leaving Jim behind dampened her relief. As soon as she landed back at the huge marine complex, she would receive needed medical attention and then she'd find Jim's commanding officer, Breckenridge. Alex began to laugh, her shoulders shaking. Her father! She'd completely forgotten about her father. Where was he? Still in Vietnam? Stateside?

Her laughter, more out of hysteria than humor, passed. The helicopter shuddered on toward its destination, and she was relieved to think of her mother being told that Alex was alive. Her father was probably more angry over her disappearance than anything else. He didn't like unplanned events getting in the way of his precise schedule.

As Alex lifted her head, her eyes awash with tears, she set some priorities for her arrival. First, she'd ask a Red Cross official to contact her parents, then she'd get someone to hunt down Lieutenant Breckenridge. Would Jim's boss be as nasty as Captain Johnson out at the hill had been? Or would he understand what Jim had done? More than anything, Alex didn't want to see Jim slapped in the brig and held on desertion charges.

"Miss Vance? I'm Lieutenant Matt Breckenridge. I understand you wanted to see me."

Alex was lying with her eyes closed on a bed in one of the MASH-unit tents. Two hours had passed since her arrival at Da Nang.

Struggling to sit up, wearing only a light blue gown of coarse cotton, Alex crossed her legs beneath the bed covers. The recon officer standing at the foot of her bed was in his mid-twenties, his dark brown hair cut very short. He was tall and lean, but not rawboned like Jim. It was his gray, hawklike eyes that made her understand why recons were set apart from the regular marine forces. For a moment, Alex was frightened by the officer's emotionless expression. And then, as if he sensed her apprehension, his eyes thawed and grew warm. His mouth stretched into a slight smile of welcome. Her left arm in a sling, Alex maneuvered awkwardly upright, and tried to return the smile.

The lieutenant carried his utility cap carelessly in his left hand. The web belt around his waist had the same items as Jim's, with the addition of a .45 pistol. As Alex searched the officer's hard features, she felt hope.

"You're Jim McKenzie's boss?"

"Yes, ma'am, I am. I understand Jim's alive?"

Alex saw worry and concern in the marine's eyes. "He's recovering from a broken leg, Lieutenant. Please, if you've got a few minutes, I've got to tell you what happened to Jim. It's important you know the truth—I'm afraid they'll put him in the brig when he gets to Da Nang."

"What?" Breckenridge muttered, coming around the end of the bed. "Jim? In the brig? What are you talking about?"

As weary as Alex was, she pointed to a nearby chair. "Sit down, Lieutenant. I've got a lot to tell you." She glanced at her watch. Her father was due to arrive from Saigon in another hour. "And I don't have much time."

Breckenridge nodded and straddled the chair. "What's going on?" he demanded.

"What do you think the Marine Corps will do with Jim now that you know the whole story?" Alex asked in a hushed voice, closely watching the officer's expression.

Breckenridge rose tensely. "McKenzie's one of the best men I've served with in the recons," he muttered more to himself than her. "He's not a coward or a deserter."

Alex watched Breckenridge pace, feeling strongly that he was a fighter—a defender of the men on his team. Alex liked the young officer. It was obvious he was loyal to his men. "I found out through Gunny Whitman that Captain Johnson, the company commander on that hill, is going to put Jim on report for disobeying a direct order from a superior officer. Jim refused to pick up a rifle and fight."

Rubbing his chin, Breckenridge nodded. "That's going to work against him."

"But he was helping with the wounded and taking ammo to the marines in the trenches. I saw him!"

Matt shook his head and glanced over at her. "How much do you know about the Marine Corps?"

"I have two brothers in the corps."

"Then you know how they feel about a marine who commits treason, deserts or refuses a direct order."

Alex nodded. "Oh, Lieutenant, you understand why he made that decision!"

"Yes, I do. I was there when Kim was killed." He shook his head. "It was a shame. A crying shame. Kim loved Jim and vice versa. What Duc did—" He took in a deep, ragged breath and gave Alex an apologetic glance. "Sorry. When things like that happen, you don't get over them fast...maybe never."

Alex understood completely. She saw how shaken the officer had become discussing Kim's death. Gently, Alex asked, "What do you think they'll do to Jim?"

Matt snorted softly and stared down the row of bunks filled with wounded marines. He kept his voice low. "Honestly? Probably slap him in leg irons and put him in the brig. I'm sure they'll charge him with insubordination at the very least. He's likely to get a court-martial."

Wincing, Alex forced the question out of her mouth. "What about prison? Will they put Jim in prison?"

Breckenridge shrugged. "I don't know. So much depends on whether and how McKenzie defends his actions. Captain Johnson is a hard-nose, from what I hear through the grapevine."

"Please, can you help Jim?"

The officer smiled slightly. "I'll get over to CID— the Central Intelligence Division—and see what I can find out."

"You're on his side, aren't you?"

"Yes, I am."

Relief flowed through Alex. "Thank God."

"Look, you need some rest, Miss Vance. You've been through a lot."

Touched by his concern, she shook her head. "Jim is more important to me, Lieutenant. He's a good man who was caught in a terrible situation. He needs everyone who's on his side working for him right now."

Settling the utility cap on his head, Breckenridge grinned sourly. "You're Jim's ace in the hole. You're a congressman's daughter. If I were you, I'd play the publicity angle for all it's worth."

Alex nodded. "I don't know how my father will react to Jim's problem. I'm hoping he'll see that Jim saved my life and forgive him for his choice."

"Your father's a hawk," Breckenridge whispered with a frown. "He's gung ho."

"I know...." Alex lifted her hand in farewell to the marine officer and watched him move quietly down the aisle toward the exit. She knew Matt Breckenridge would defend Jim. Would her father? Anxiety coursed through Alex as she lay back down. Sleep, as badly as she needed it, refused to come. Her emotions skewed sharply from worry for Jim on that heavily defended hill and her father's arrival. What would her father do once he heard her story? Would he help defend Jim or try to put him behind bars?

"Alex," Hiram Vance said heavily from where he sat on the chair next to her bed, "I think you're suffering from all the trauma you endured. McKenzie may have saved your life, but the boy's a damned coward and a shirker, in my opinion."

"No!" Alex's cry sheared through the tent. "No!" she whispered stridently, "he's not!" Sitting up, her arm aching with pain, Alex held her father's dark stare. At fifty, Hiram Vance had silver streaks in his black hair. He was dressed in a suit, of all things, looking sorely out of place in the humid jungle climate. But Alex knew he was proud of the power he wielded in Congress—particularly of being a member of the prestigious finance committee.

Holding up his square hands, Vance gave her a look of disapproval. "Alex, you're distraught from the experience. Now, settle down. Getting all upset isn't going to accomplish a thing."

Alex tried to bridle her emotions. "But Father, Jim saved my life! Isn't that worth something?"

"Of course it is. But it doesn't take away from the fact that he refused a superior officer's order under fire. And I hear from CID that he deserted his recon team."

"He didn't desert! How could he go anywhere with a broken leg?"

"Look, this isn't your fight. It isn't even your business, Alex. You're a civilian who happened to get caught in the crossfire."

Alex glared at her father. "Well, what are you going to do now that you know Jim's a conscientious objector?"

"I'm going to do nothing. The marines can handle a yellow-bellied coward like McKenzie without my involvement." He rose and smoothed the dark fabric of his suit against his protruding belly. "Now, stop worrying about this jerk and get some rest, Alex. I'm going to talk to the doctor about getting you flown to Saigon for some decent treatment. You need to get out of this country. You're distraught."

Tears welled into Alex's eyes as she looked up at her father's grim features. "No," she quavered, "I'm not going anywhere until I know what the Marine Corps is going to do with Jim McKenzie."

He halted and stared at her. "Alexandra, what's gotten into you? Do you still have a fever?"

She wanted to cry, but didn't dare. Every time she got emotional in front of her father, he walked away from her, as if she wasn't worthy of his attention. Clamping down on the cauldron of emotions roiling within her, she rasped, "My fever's gone, Father. I've got enough antibiotics in me to kill a horse. My shrapnel wound is fine. I'm clear-headed."

"Sweetie pie, don't concern yourself with this McKenzie fellow. He's trying to change his mind in midstream. This conscientious objector routine is just a cover to get out of doing his duty. Let the corps handle it and let's get you home."

Her heart jagged with anger and fear. "Father, I'm staying. I'm over eighteen, and I decide where and when I'm leaving Da Nang. I spent a week with that man, and he's one of the most courageous and kind human beings I've ever met. I'm not abandoning him when he needs me."

He stared down at her. "Alex, you obey me."

Alex held his glare. Rarely had she stood up to her father about anything—except her degree in nursing. "I will not."

"You're being disrespectful to my wishes."

Alex's eyes widened. Her voice strangled with anger, she said, "If it was Case or Buck, you'd be slapping them on the back for making a command decision. But since it's me doing it, you think I'm being disrespectful."

"Young lady, you are way out of line."

Alex heard the tremor in his voice as it grew deep and defensive. "A man's life is at stake, Father, and I'm not letting him down," she continued heedlessly. "He saved my life. I'll be damned if I'm going to let the Marine Corps railroad him! Jim has every reason never to fire a rifle again!"

With a curse, Vance shook his finger at her. "Alexandra, you stay out of this!"

"No." For a moment, as she watched her father's square face turn a purple hue, Alex wondered if he was going to reach out and strike her. It wouldn't be the first time, although her brothers had been struck many more times than she had, growing up. Hiram Vance was known on the Hill for his short-fused temper, his opinionated stance and his bellicose personality. He was even more single-minded when dealing with his family. Alex watched his hands slowly ball into fists. Would he hit her in front of all these marines?

Her mouth dry, Alex held her father's black glare. She watched as he flexed his fists. The rage in his face was consummate, and inwardly, Alex tried to steel herself for his explosive tirade. Jim had faced the enemy for her—he'd risked his life to get her sulfa drugs and take her to the firebase. She could do no less for him now.

"This isn't the time or place to correct you," he rasped, glancing at the tent full of wounded marines, most of whom were now watching the confrontation with open curiosity. "What are your plans?" Hiram ground out.

Alex set her mouth, and her eyes narrowed. "To help Jim any way I can."

He advanced upon Alex, towering threateningly above her. "Young lady, under no circumstances will you embarrass me. Do you understand?"

Refusing even to wince, Alex held her father's stare. He had always been overly worried about public opinion, but then, Alex reminded herself bitterly, her father was a politician. They had to be responsive to the public. "Whatever I decide to do will be on my own," she said, hoping the quaver in her voice wasn't obvious. "I'll leave your name out of it."

Her father whirled around and stalked out of the tent.

Alex released a ragged sigh. The marine in the next bed, his leg in a suspended cast, gave a soft whistle. She looked over at him. He couldn't have been more than eighteen.

"Man, that was some kind of stand you took, Miss Vance."

Alex heard the admiration in the marine's voice. Shaking visibly, she lay back down and shut her eyes. Her entire world was coming apart. It had been no surprise that her father didn't see Jim in the same light that she did. As Alex lay there, trying to pull herself together for the coming fight to save Jim, she knew in her heart that this argument with her father was only the beginning. Hiram Vance prided himself on winning—on always having the last word. This was only the second time in her life she'd stood up to her powerful father.

Alex's shoulder ached badly, but her heart hurt worse. Between her father and Jim was a chasm. How could Jim be so sensitive, gentle and thoughtful when her father was the opposite? Finally Alex drifted into a restless sleep, where she dreamed of Jim McKenzie, of his soft smile, the teasing light in his dark blue eyes and his incredibly gentle touch. A fierce love blanketed Alex, her sleep deepened, and in her dreams she saw them together—and happy.

"Corporal McKenzie, you're under arrest for desertion and insubordination to a superior officer."

Jim stood in the headquarters tent of Da Nang, brig guards on either side of him as Major Dover read the charges. Exhaustion lapped at him, but he stood at attention the best he could with his aching leg. Yesterday he'd taken off the makeshift splint because it was falling apart.

The door to the tent was jerked open. Lieutenant Matt Breckenridge entered, his face set and grim as he approached Jim.

"Major, what's going on? I understand my man just returned from that hill. He's in need of medical attention."

DOUBLE YOUR ACTION PLAY...

"ROLL A DOUBLE!"

Peel off label & place inside

**CLAIM UP TO 4 BOOKS
PLUS A LOVELY
"KEY TO YOUR HEART"
PENDANT NECKLACE**

ABSOLUTELY FREE!

SEE INSIDE..

NO RISK, NO OBLIGATION TO BUY...NOW OR EVER!

GUARANTEED

PLAY "ROLL A DOUBLE" AND GET AS MANY AS FIVE GIFTS!

HERE'S HOW TO PLAY:

1. Peel off label from front cover. Place it in space provided at right. With a coin, carefully scratch off the silver dice. This makes you eligible to receive two or more free books, and possibly another gift, depending on what is revealed beneath the scratch-off area.

2. You'll receive brand-new Silhouette Special Edition® novels. When you return this card, we'll rush you the books and gift you qualify for ABSOLUTELY FREE!

3. Then, if we don't hear from you, every month, we'll send you 6 additional novels to read and enjoy. You can return them and owe nothing, but if you decide to keep them, you'll pay only $2.96 per book—a saving of 43¢ each off the cover price.

4. When you subscribe to the Silhouette Reader Service™, you'll also get our newsletter, as well as additional free gifts from time to time.

5. You must be completely satisfied. You may cancel at any time simply by sending us a note or a shipping statement marked "cancel" or by returning any shipment to us at our expense.

The Austrian crystal sparkles like a diamond! And it's carefully set in a romantic "Key to Your Heart" pendant on a generous 18" chain. The entire necklace is yours free as added thanks for giving our Reader Service a try!

"ROLL A DOUBLE!"

PLACE LABEL HERE

SCRATCH HERE

SEE CLAIM CHART BELOW

235 CIS AELS
(U-SIL-SE-05/92)

YES! I have placed my label from the front cover into the space provided above and scratched off the silver dice. Please rush me the free books and gift that I am entitled to. I understand that I am under no obligation to purchase any books, as explained on the opposite page.

NAME _____

ADDRESS _____ APT. _____

CITY _____ STATE _____ ZIP CODE _____

CLAIM CHART

🎲🎲	**4 FREE BOOKS PLUS FREE "KEY TO YOUR HEART" NECKLACE**	
🎲🎲	**3 FREE BOOKS**	
🎲🎲	**2 FREE BOOKS**	

CLAIM NO. 37-829

SILHOUETTE "NO RISK" GUARANTEE

- You're not required to buy a single book—ever!
- You must be completely satisfied or you may cancel at any time simply by sending us a note or shipping statement marked "cancel" or by returning any shipment to us at our cost. Either way, you will receive no more books; you'll have no obligation to buy.
- The free books and gift you claimed on this "Roll A Double" offer remain yours to keep no matter what you decide.

If offer card is missing, please write to: Silhouette Reader Service, 3010 Walden Ave., P.O. Box 1867, Buffalo, NY 14269-1867

DETACH AND MAIL CARD TODAY!

BUSINESS REPLY MAIL

FIRST CLASS MAIL   PERMIT NO. 717   BUFFALO, NY

POSTAGE WILL BE PAID BY ADDRESSEE

SILHOUETTE READER SERVICE
3010 WALDEN AVE
PO BOX 1867
BUFFALO NY 14240-9952

NO POSTAGE
NECESSARY
IF MAILED
IN THE
UNITED STATES

Dover glanced at Breckenridge. "Captain Johnson on Hill 223 put your man on charges for his actions during a recent firefight, Lieutenant." He handed him the orders. "Before you get your hackles up, I suggest you read this."

Jim glanced at Breckenridge, relief flowing through him. Two days had passed before the hill had been secured from the attacking VC. The only thing on Jim's mind now was Alex. How was she? He knew Captain Johnson would slap him in leg irons as soon as possible. Jim had already resigned himself to his fate. He saw his lieutenant's face grow hard.

"Major Dover, I request that Corporal McKenzie be given over to me. I'll be responsible for him while he's here in Da Nang awaiting court-martial."

"Sorry, Lieutenant, but that's not in the rule book. Corporal McKenzie is going straight to the brig here on base to await deposition of this matter."

Breckenridge glared at the officer. "With all due respect, sir, Corporal McKenzie suffered a broken leg while on patrol. Look at him. He's got other wounds. I demand he be taken to the MASH unit first to be cared for."

Dover shrugged. "Fine. He's your responsibility in that arena, Lieutenant. Get him medical attention, then these brig guards will escort him to his cell. Those are my orders. Do you understand, Lieutenant?"

"They're perfectly clear, sir." Breckenridge looked over at Jim. "Let's go," he ordered softly.

Limping badly, Jim followed, the brig guards remaining close by. They left the tent, the hot sun feeling good to Jim. He took a deep, steadying breath of air.

"I'm glad to see you, sir."

Breckenridge looked at him grimly. "Same here, Jim. I'm afraid you're not going to find too many friendly faces here in Da Nang. In fact, Miss Vance and I are your only supporters."

"What about Miss Vance? Is she okay?" Jim asked.

"Yeah, she's going to be fine."

"Did they ship her out?" Jim hoped so.

"No. She's remaining at the base in Da Nang." Breckenridge glanced over at him sharply. "You've got two people who know you're not a deserter or a coward, McKenzie—me and her."

"What are you talking about?"

"Alex Vance is refusing to leave Da Nang until you're cleared of all charges. She's a witness, if you will, in your defense." Matt pursed his lips. "I've already talked to the CID people to see what charges are being pressed by this Captain Johnson."

Jim nodded. "Yes, sir." His heart somersaulted with joy and pain. "Alex is really staying here?"

"Waiting to see you."

If only he could see Alex one last time. "Sir, could you let her know I'm at the MASH unit gettin' patched up?"

A slight thaw came to Breckenridge's narrowed eyes. "She's at the same unit you're going to. I'll make sure she knows you've arrived."

"Thank you, sir." Jim had spent a year with Matt Breckenridge and his recon team. He knew the officer was an honorable man with clear-cut values. "I'm sorry to put you in this jam, sir."

Breckenridge smiled briefly. "Don't be."

Jim stared at the officer. "I refuse to pick up a rifle again, sir."

"I know that." The lieutenant's mouth compressed. "We each have our limit. You reached yours with Kim. Someday, I'll probably reach mine, too."

It meant a lot to Jim that Breckenridge didn't see him as a deserter or a coward. "Thanks for understanding, Lieutenant."

Breckenridge slowed and opened the door that led to the emergency-room facilities of the MASH unit. His gray eyes narrowed with intensity. "I'm going to do everything humanly possible to help you. But I'll tell you right now, I don't think it's going to be enough. I'm the one who's sorry. You're a good marine, and you don't deserve the way they're going to use you as a scapegoat."

Jim understood only too well. The corps had a proud tradition to uphold, and with the war starting to escalate in earnest, they didn't want a black eye in the media with a marine refusing to bear arms against the enemy. As he hobbled into the facility, greeted by nurses in green shirts and slacks, Jim knew his freedom was at an end. All he wanted—all he needed—was to see Alex one last time. He was about to ask, when Breckenridge gripped his shoulder.

"I'll go find Miss Vance for you."

Tears stung Jim's eyes and he quickly looked away from the marine officer. Breckenridge was the kind of man Jim would have died for, if necessary. The fact that the officer would put his career on the line to defend Jim was simply amazing. Breckenridge understood why Jim could never pick up a rifle again. And so did Alex. But they were the only two people in the world who ever would.

The brig guards remained at the tent entrance, never taking their eyes off Jim as a doctor and nurse maneuvered him around on a gurney. He lay quietly, knowing the medical team would x-ray his leg, make a cast for it and patch up the various other wounds he'd gotten in the past couple days on that godforsaken hill.

Tiredness lapped at him. As they wheeled him down the hall to the X-ray room, he closed his eyes. Like everyone else, he'd only gotten snatches of sleep in the last forty-eight hours. In moments, Jim spiraled into an exhausted slumber, oblivious to the building storm that surrounded him.

Chapter Eight

Jim was jolted awake as they wheeled him out of X ray and back to the emergency room. To his surprise, he saw Alex waiting for him, draped in a long, light blue cotton robe, her left arm in a clean white sling. Jim couldn't hide his reaction to her. Even though the brig guards were watching him, disgust written on their every feature, and his skipper was there, too, Jim couldn't control the gamut of emotions rushing through him.

Alex's gray eyes shone with love, the welcome in them undeniable. Jim sat up. He wanted to protect her from himself, from what he knew was going to happen to him.

"Jim?"

He winced inwardly, the quaver in her low voice tearing at him. As she drew near his gurney and held out her hand, he took it.

A lump formed in his throat. "How you doin', gal?"

"Okay. I was worried sick for you. I heard the VC almost took back the hill." She choked back a sob. "I had these horrible dreams that you might be killed."

The ache to sweep her into his arms was overwhelming. Just the feminine strength of her fingers made him want to cry. Clearing his throat, Jim forced a slight, one-cornered smile for her benefit. "I made it back alive, that's all that counts. Look at you, all gussied up. Your hair's washed. I didn't realize it had gold threads of sunlight in it."

Jim sat up on the gurney, still dressed in his filthy, foul-smelling clothes. Alex realized that he was beyond exhaustion, his eyes red-rimmed and dark. He desperately needed a bath, some sleep and some food. His face appeared even more gaunt than she recalled. She rallied beneath his teasing. She wanted badly to reach over and kiss him but didn't dare under the circumstances.

"What are they going to do with you?"

Jim glanced over at Breckenridge. "After they make a cast for this leg of mine, they're taking me to the brig."

"No!" It was an animal-like cry. Alex whirled around and pinned Breckenridge with a pleading look.

"How can they do that, Lieutenant? Jim saved my life! Doesn't that count for anything?"

Matt walked over to where she stood. "I'm doing everything I can to help him, Miss Vance," he assured her.

"But," she whispered distractedly, "his leg."

"If he walked in here under his own power, the major figures he can walk over to the brig and stay there instead of here at the hospital," Breckenridge said unhappily. "I'm sorry."

Alex saw the genuine regret in the officer's eyes. She turned back to Jim, her grip on his hand tight. "I'm going to help you, Jim. I swear I will."

"Listen to me, gal, no one can help me now. The best thing you can do is board the next freedom bird out of here and go Stateside. Go back to the real world and forget about me." It hurt to say those words, especially when he didn't mean them. The stubbornness he saw in Alex's face told him she wasn't going to listen anyway.

"No! The way they're treating you—treating this whole situation—is *inhumane!* I won't stand for it, Jim."

Reaching up, desperate now, Jim placed his hands lightly on her small shoulders. "Listen to me, Alex. The corps deals with men such as myself in its own way. There's no use trying to defend me. It won't work."

Tears glimmered in her eyes. "Like hell it won't," she quavered unsteadily. "I'm not giving up on you, Jim. You may have given up on yourself, but I haven't!"

Desperation fueled his unraveling feelings. "Alex, go home! Forget about me, about what happened here in Nam!"

Alex pulled out of his grasp, breathing raggedly. Glaring at the lieutenant and then back at him, she rasped, "You don't forsake the one you love, Jim McKenzie! You're stuck with me! I'm not going to abandon you!" She whirled away, walked toward the double swinging doors and disappeared through them.

Jim glanced over at his skipper. "Can't you convince her, sir?"

Breckenridge shrugged and came over. In a low voice, he ordered the brig guards to wait outside. When they were alone, he asked, "Is it true? You two love each other?"

Hanging his head, Jim worked to stop the feelings he wanted so desperately to own and, more importantly, to share with Alex. The whole situation was impossible. "Sir, I do love her. I don't know when or how it happened, it just did." Raising his head, he held the officer's saddened eyes. "You know as well as I do that it won't work. They're gonna throw me in prison. It doesn't matter what my story is, the corps is going to punish me. She's fallen in love with the wrong person. Do you understand that, Skipper? I've gotta stop her from ruining her life by loving me."

Breckenridge nodded and stepped aside as the doctor, dressed in a green top and pants, swung through the doors with X rays in hand. "I understand, Jim. First things first. Let's get this leg of yours in a cast."

Alex finished dressing in a newly purchased pair of white cotton slacks and a pale gold blouse. A private tent had been loaned to her while she remained at the base. Since seeing Jim the other day, Alex had taken things into her own hands. Luckily, she'd left her purse and other valuables behind in Da Nang before climbing onto that fateful helicopter flight. She had money to remain in Vietnam for some time.

Her father was in Saigon, conferring, she supposed, with the military leaders on political issues. Alex had left her address and phone number with his hotel in case he wanted to get hold of her. Until then, she was moving ahead with her plans. She opened the tent door.

"Miss Vance?"

"Hi, Lieutenant Breckenridge." Alex stepped aside and smiled. "Please, come in."

Breckenridge took off his utility cap and halted just inside the door. He smiled tiredly. "This place looks a lot better than the hospital. Glad they were able to put you up here."

Shutting the door, Alex motioned the recon marine to sit down on a metal folding chair. "It is," she agreed.

Matt sat opposite her. "Jim's been back two days now, and I've got to tell you, all hell's starting to break loose."

Alex halted and stared down at the officer. "Because I gave the U.S. reporters my story of how Jim saved my life?"

"Yes, ma'am."

"If it will help Jim, I'll continue to give interviews to bring attention to his case, Lieutenant."

"I think it's helping already. At least CID has dropped the desertion charges against him. That was the worse of the two charges—the one that could put him before a firing squad."

Relief made her dizzy, and Alex whispered, "Oh, thank God." She saw the happiness in the officer's eyes, too. "I suppose they want me to shut up and disappear so they can get on with trying to hang Jim on insubordination charges, then."

Moving the utility cap slowly through his scarred, callused fingers, Breckenridge watched as she paced back and forth. "They'd probably breathe easier, Miss Vance—"

"Call me Alex, please." She halted and tried to smile but failed. "I'm so glad you're on Jim's side, Lieutenant."

He nodded. "Alex, Jim asked me to come over here and talk some sense into you—his words, not mine."

Her heart began pounding painfully and she sat down on the cot.

"McKenzie and I both know he's going to be in for a rough ride for refusing to pick up a rifle. The corps will hang him on that, even if they can't make the desertion charges stick. Jim's worried about you, what this press might do because your father's a congressman."

Alex touched her aching brow. "It's just like him to be worried for me and not for himself." She glanced up at Matt. "That's why I love him. He's honest and sincere—not like so many other guys I've met."

"Yes," Breckenridge agreed, "McKenzie's all of that. Look, he wants you to get on with your life and forget him."

"How can I?"

Breckenridge shrugged. "I don't know. I can see you love him. But..."

"What?"

"You only knew each other for seven days under some very trying circumstances."

"Love doesn't have a time limit," Alex snapped back, getting up and starting to pace again. "Are those his words or your observation?"

"Mine," the officer admitted unhappily.

Alex stopped and stood tensely before the marine lieutenant. "Nothing you can say will make me change my mind. I'm going to keep giving interviews to any news reporter who wants the story of Jim's bravery. If not for him, I'd be dead. That's what the Marine Corps is so conveniently overlooking."

"They aren't overlooking it, Alex. What they are focusing in on is the fact that if they don't slap McKenzie with a stiff penalty for refusing orders under fire, other marines might get the same idea."

She shook her head. "Maybe that wouldn't be such a bad idea. War is no place for anyone, Lieutenant."

"I can't disagree," he whispered.

"So what I'm hearing is that Jim's a scapegoat? A sacrificial lamb because he stood up for his own values and morals?"

"Yes," Breckenridge said wearily. "The court-martial board is convening tomorrow morning, Alex. It's closed to all but key military personnel."

"Don't they want me as a witness?"

He shook his head.

Alex shut her eyes. "My God, how did the military get such blanket authority? This goes beyond our constitutional laws."

Breckenridge got up and walked over to her. He laid his hand on her shoulder. "If it makes you feel any better, the newspaper articles here in country and back in the States will probably force the convening board officers to give Jim a much lighter sentence than Captain Johnson wanted."

Tears swam in Alex's eyes as she looked up at Breckenridge. She realized he was suffering no less for Jim than she was. "What are you trying to say? That his sentence and where they're going to send him have already been determined?"

"I believe," Matt said with an effort, "they'll probably reduce him to private and give him six months in Long Binh jail. It's located near Saigon. I don't think anyone wants Jim Stateside where peace demonstrators can march in his behalf. If I can read between the lines of the colonel in charge, he wants to sweep this whole thing under the rug and hope it goes away. By keeping Jim in country, under guard where no one from the media can reach him, they figure the real world will eventually forget him."

Alex wavered. She felt the officer grip her shoulder, as if to support her after delivering the news. Alex drew in a ragged breath. "I don't have the kind of money it would take to hire a civilian lawyer back in the States to help. I wished I did, but Father and I don't get along very well. He pays only my nursing-school tuition. I work two part-time jobs to cover my rent and living expenses.''

''Alex, you've done what you can. When this court-martial comes up for review, I believe the decision against Jim will be overturned. Maybe you weren't aware of the required review process, but it's Jim's best chance at vindication. The local command is too close to the fighting, and Captain Johnson's embellishment of the refusal under fire conditions is hurting Jim's chance at a fair hearing. No lawyer is going to be able to help him right now. Look, Jim wants you to go back home.'' Matt took an envelope from the pocket of his utilities. ''I managed to smuggle in paper and a pen to him. He wanted to write you. You won't be able to see him again.''

Alex felt as if her heart was breaking. A sob escaped her. ''I won't be able to see him?''

''No...I'm sorry. Once they sentence Jim, they'll put him in leg irons and fly him down to Long Binh.''

Anger and grief surged through her. ''H-how can you handle this so calmly?''

''Because I'm resolved to the fact that this is one case that can be won more easily on appeal than in the present kangaroo-court mentality,'' Breckenridge told her grimly.

''Aren't you upset over the unfairness of it?''

''Of course. I have contacted some people who will be able to assist me in the appeal hearing for Jim.''

Alex took the letter. The pages were smudged with perspiration and dust. What kind of conditions were there at the brig? Alex was afraid to ask in the wake of all the bad news.

"I think Jim's wrong about one thing," Breckenridge murmured. "He believes your love for him is a passing thing, created out of the trauma you survived in the jungle." Matt turned the envelope over. "I took the liberty of finding out the mailing address for Long Binh—just in case you want to stay in touch."

Tears streamed down Alex's cheeks. Pressing her hand against her lips, she nodded. "Th-thank you, Lieutenant. You're a good man. Jim is lucky to have you during all this."

The officer settled his cap back on his head. "No," he whispered, "Jim is lucky to have *you*. As it stands, the corps is going to treat him like a model prisoner, knowing that you're out there monitoring his whereabouts, his state of mind and health."

"D-do you think they'll allow Jim to get my letters?"

With a shrug, Matt said, "I don't know. By law, they have to let him get mail."

"What if I don't get answers? How will I know if he's receiving my mail at all, or if he's just refusing to answer it?"

Matt shook his head unhappily. "There's no way to know. Look, I'll be seeing Jim. I'm one of the few people who can get to him with the tight security over this whole deal. Maybe you'd like to read his letter and write one yourself. I can at least carry a letter from you back to him."

Dashing away the tears, Alex moved to the small desk. "Yes, I'll do that. Thanks, Matt."

He smiled offhandedly and walked around the tent. At the door he sighed. "You know, if the wife, girlfriend or children of a marine need anything, fellow marines will pitch in and help. It's an unspoken camaraderie, if you will."

Taking out a sheaf of stationery from a drawer, Alex looked at Breckenridge. His profile appeared harshly chiseled against the sunlight pouring through the screen door. "I don't know what I can ever do to thank you for helping Jim and me."

Matt looked over his shoulder at her. "I hope you understand that Captain Johnson isn't the best example of a Marine Corps officer, as far as I'm concerned. Jim is one of the finest marines I've ever commanded. There's a gut honesty in him that I've seen in very few men. He's straightforward, intelligent, and he has an unbending loyalty to his friends."

"I know," Alex said softly. "I was on the receiving end of that care. That's why he deserves my best effort—my courage, not my cowardice."

"He's a lucky man. I hope he knows that."

With shaky hands, Alex unfolded the letter. Jim's scrawl was nearly illegible, and she recalled him telling her how much trouble he had learning to read and write in school. Hungrily, she absorbed his handwritten note.

Dear Alexandra,

I'm asking Lieutenant Breckenridge to hand deliver this letter to you. I'm doing okay. At least my leg's stopped hurting me. I'm getting used to the cast. It seems that the word goin' around is I'm gonna get sent to Long Binh here in Vietnam. That's not too bad. I told my skipper I'd get real good at busting rocks with a sixteen-pound sledgehammer.

I want to thank you for all your help. My skipper said you stirred up a hornet's nest out there on my behalf. Right now, my worry is for you. Please go home. You've done all you can for me, and I'm grateful. If you could do me one favor and visit my ma and pa, I'd be beholden. They don't have a phone, so you'd have to drive up to see them. I hope this isn't asking too much, but I know how worried they'll be. My skipper's writing them a long letter of explanation. Could you deliver it to them? Tell them the truth of what happened? I'm worried my pa might think I'm a coward. Tell him I'm sorry I've caused him such shame. I didn't mean to.

Go home and go back to learning to be a nurse. You'll make a great one. Forget about me, gal. I'm worthless compared to some college guy you'll meet, fall in love with and marry someday. You deserve better than me. When you get home, you'll see the wisdom of my words. Take care. I'll never forget you, Alexandra. You're as purty as your name.

Your friend forever,
Jim McKenzie

"Oh, God." Alex choked and pushed the letter away. Burying her face in her hands, she began to cry. A moment later, she felt Breckenridge's hands on her shaking shoulders.

Sniffing, Alex said brokenly, "I'm okay. Really, I am. Just let me write him a letter."

Jim lifted his head from where he sat in his small cell when he heard the door at the end of the facility open and close. Light was low, the humidity high, and the smell of sweat hung in the air. His cot was long, narrow and uncomfortable. Out of the shadowy gloom he recognized Lieutenant Breckenridge being escorted by a brig chaser. Swinging his leg over the cot, being careful not to crack the plaster cast on the iron chains that held the cot against the wall, Jim stood.

The clanking of the keys in the lock, the protesting screech of the iron-bar door opening and closing, filled the sour-smelling air. Jim remained tense and quiet until the brig chaser left for his station at the end of the passageway.

Matt gestured for him to sit down. Keeping his voice very low, he pulled out a white envelope and handed it to Jim.

"From Alex."

With a nod, his heart doing double time in his chest, Jim carefully opened the letter, his hands trembling. He hadn't expected a response, and joy poured through him, momentarily erasing the sadness that had hung with him since he'd returned to Da Nang.

Alex's handwriting was small and flowery, so very feminine in comparison to his large, almost unreadable scrawl. Jim glanced over at his skipper.

"Was she able to read my letter at all?"

Matt smiled. "Yes."

"I don't know how. It looked like hen scratchin' in the barnyard."

"I think," Matt added, "that loving you as much as she does, she could read anything you wrote."

Jim's heart thudded hard in his chest. He held Breckenridge's wry look and then hungrily began to read her letter.

Dear Jim,

It was such a relief to know you're all right. Lieutenant Breckenridge has been wonderful about explaining all that's happened. And yes, I will go see your parents and deliver his letter as soon as I get home. That's a promise. I'm sure your father won't be ashamed of you. I know I'm not. I'm proud of you, Jim. Proud you have the courage of your convictions, proud of your honesty, morals and values. I stand behind you all the way.

Matt said you would probably be at Long Binh for imprisonment. He gave me your address, so I'll be writing to you. Jim, I love you. You can't tell me to go away and forget you. What I feel for you, even if it was born out of the wartime situation, is real. I'm not going home to forget what we shared or what you mean to me. I know you love me, too. I saw it in your eyes every time you looked at me. I'm willing to let time test our relationship. I'll be waiting for you. I love you— forever.

                                        Alexandra

"Lordy," Jim whispered, his hand clenching the letter.

"What?"

He glanced over at Breckenridge. "That woman's got the stubbornness of the worst Missouri mule I've ever known."

With a grin, the lieutenant said, "You deserve Alex Vance whether you know it or not."

"Sir, you know what kind of life I could offer her. I'm a hill boy. She's the daughter of a congressman. She's got book learnin': We're from different sides of the track. Why doesn't she see that?"

"I guess because she sees the good in you, Jim, like I do. Economic level, education or where you live has nothing to do with what you are inside." Breckenridge shook his head. "I hope like hell my morals and values are never asked to be tested as yours have been. I'd like to think I could stand up for my convictions the way you have."

"I never thought my time in the corps would end like this. I wanted to make my pa proud of me...."

"Alex said she'll talk to your folks. I'm sure that, between my letter and her explanation, your father will understand." Breckenridge gave him an appraising look. "You love her?"

"Yes, sir."

Placing his hands on his hips, the officer sighed. "I hope you can overcome your own prejudice about Alex and write back to her, then. She'll be writing to you."

Unhappy, Jim bowed his head. He stared at the pristine white paper in the gloom of his cell. "I—I don't know if I can. I'm sure once she gets back to the States, this intense love she feels for me will go away."

Breckenridge came over and patted Jim's shoulder. "You're afraid of losing her, aren't you? You're not really doubting her love at all."

With a nod, Jim shut his eyes. "She's too purty, too special, Lieutenant. How can someone like Alexandra love me? She's like a dream. I have no bloodlines, no money. My folks are poor. Once she gets back to her own kind, she'll forget about me."

The lieutenant gripped his shoulder. "I don't have the answers you need, Jim. Maybe the letters you share with each other will help. You two need time anyway, to get to know each other better. Perhaps something good will come out of this, after all. I hope for your sakes it does. You deserve to be happy after all the hell you've gone through."

Tears leaked into Jim's tightly shut eyes. He wanted to cry for himself and for Alex. Lieutenant Breckenridge left, and Jim sat alone in the gloom. Despair settled around him. Tomorrow, he'd be sentenced at the court-martial and hauled in chains down to Long Binh. Would Alex write once she got back to the States? Or, as his weeping heart was already warning him, would she forget him?

Chapter Nine

Dear Alex,

By now, Lieutenant Breckenridge has probably gotten ahold of you—he promised he would—to tell you about my court-martial and sentencing. My mail can be censored, and there are a lot of things I can't write about now that I'm in Long Binh. I'm doing as well as can be expected. I wonder when you'll receive this letter.

My leg is much better, but the doc said even if I wanted to go back into combat, I couldn't 'cause I chipped one of the bones and it won't stand for the kind of punishment a recon would put on it. He said that heavy construction work was out for me, too. Guess I'd better change my idea of careers, huh? I had thought of going home and apprenticing as a construction worker after my tour was up. I like working with my hands. A lot of hill folk go down to the city and work in the walnut factory where they make bowls and other wood products for the tourists. I don't know if I want to spend the rest of my life cutting and shaping bowls from walnut wood.

How are you doing? Is your shoulder healing? I think about you a lot. Lieutenant Breckenridge mentioned you went round and round with your father, and that he was het up. That's Missouri slang for being angry. I hope you've made peace with him and you're now back getting ready to graduate after summer school.

I really don't expect you to write, Alex. I just wanted to let you know I'm well and things will settle down now that I'm in prison. They gave me four months, a bad conduct discharge, busted me down to private and fined me. Aside from that, I'm alive. I want you to go on and live your life and forget about what happened here in Nam. You deserve only the best. I got a letter from Ma the other day, and she said you came to visit them right after you got Stateside. For that, I owe you plenty, gal. Her letter made me cry. They forgave me for my decision. Even my pa, who can't write much at all (he only had sixth-grade book learnin'), penned me a few lines. I don't know what you did, Alex, but whatever it was, they think I'm some kind of hero instead of an undesirable jailbird. Thank you, gal. You're the kindest, purtiest lady I've ever met, and I pray for your happiness back in the real world.

Your friend,
Jim McKenzie

Alex sat curled up on the small sofa in the apartment she shared with two other nursing students. Tears blurred Jim's handwritten pages. His white stationery was stained with sweat and dirt smudges. Outside the apartment, the June breeze barely moved the yellow curtains that framed the window.

Another letter, this one from Lieutenant Breckenridge, had arrived two days earlier. Alex reached down and opened it up again, her stomach twisting with fear for Jim.

Dear Alex,
Jim McKenzie was sentenced to four months at hard-rock labor at Long Binh jail, down near Saigon. I had hoped he'd get less of a sentence, but the local military machine wasn't going to show much leniency. The appointed counsel for Jim told me after the sentencing that two years had been talked about earlier. The counsel felt all your work, the publicity and the threat of further media spotlighting of Jim's case forced them to give him a "light" sentence. Right now, I'm in the midst of an appeal process for him. It will be slow, but Jim is worth fighting for.

What Jim won't be able to tell you are the conditions he'll be under at Long Binh. Deserters, malingerers (men who maim or injure themselves on purpose to get out of combat duty) and AWOL individuals are housed at this facility. All the mail is read by censors. Further, Jim can't say anything "bad" about his jailers, the jail itself, his living conditions, or anything that might be viewed as a negative. You're really going to have to read between the lines of his letters to glean the truth.

I'm sure Jim will get his mail. I believe the military wants this whole thing to blow over and be forgotten. I don't think they'll fail to deliver your mail to Jim for fear you'll start granting more interviews.

I'll miss Jim out on recon missions. He was one of the best, and I told him so. I also realize that each of us has a limit that, once it's reached, we can't go beyond. Jim reached his. I don't see his decision as negative. I respect what he did. I just hope I don't hit my limit. I'm going back in the bush, so this is the last letter you'll get from me for a while, but I will keep you posted on the appeal's progress. However, if you do have problems getting mail to Jim, write and let me know. I'll see what I can do from my end.

Sincerely, Matt Breckenridge

Both letters lay in her lap as Alex mulled over the situation. Jim's folks were warm, simple people, and seeing them had helped heal some of her unseen wounds. It had also increased her love of Jim, and her commitment to him. Getting up, Alex moved to her study table. She was in the middle of summer school and wanted to pen Jim a long letter before she sat down to hit the books.

June 20, 1965

Dear Jim,
I hope you know how important and wonderful

it was getting your letter. I just got back from one of my summer-school classes, and your letter was waiting in my mailbox at the apartment building where I live off campus.

I realize more than you know that you can't talk about a lot of things. That's okay, I understand. I can't see you spending your life in a wood factory turning out walnut bowls, either. Why not reach for the stars? Go after something that may seem impossible but really isn't? You were so good with me when we were under fire. Your calmness, your common sense and practicality are skills not everyone has. And why think only of menial jobs when you get out of jail? You have a good head on your shoulders. How about college? I'm going to send you my college's catalog of courses. Maybe there's something in there that interests you. What about starting a correspondence course? Why let the time in jail be a waste? Let it be a concentrated period of learning, instead. I know you have to perform physical labor there, but surely you would have time to study, too.

I'm afraid my father and I aren't getting along at all. He's still "het up" over my active participation on your behalf, so we aren't talking much. I still do go home on weekends. Mom and I get along fine, and she understands my feelings. My father's a proud man with stubborn opinions. I wish he could bend, like you did, Jim. But I don't think he will. Mom says with time he will get over being angry with me.

My shoulder wound is healing well. I'm undergoing some physical therapy to get full use of it, but right now I've got about eighty percent mobility. Around school I'm a heroine, if you will. Everyone wanted to know what happened, because they'd read magazine and newspaper accounts—which I'm sending on to you—of the crash and you rescuing me. They all think it's neat, but I don't. War is a terrible thing, and I try to get them to understand that. They tend to look at me sort of funny, think I'm crazy for saying it and shrug it off.

I've talked to my college counselor, Mrs. Riddell, who was an army nurse in a medical unit during the Korean War! So far, she's the only one who understands what I'm going through. Yes, I get nightmares (I could hear you asking that question as soon as I wrote the above sentence!) and whenever I hear a car backfire or something, I wince. Or, worse, I break out in a cold sweat. Twice now I've had vivid flashes of the time we were in the jungle getting bombed by the B-52's. Mrs. Riddell told me she had similar reactions to things that happened to her in Korea. We share a commonality.

I've talked to Dr. George Fielding, the head of the psychiatric department here at the college, and asked him if these kinds of reactions had been reported by men in other wars. He got so interested in my observations of my own responses that he wants me to start compiling them. I think we're onto something, Jim. Mrs. Riddell has agreed to help me make up a questionnaire because of her combat-duty experience. I don't know where this all is leading, but I'm bound and determined to try and help our returning men adjust after this awful war.

I enjoyed my time with your parents. Your mother is so warm and outgoing—like you. Once I had told them the whole story, she cried. Your father is a kind man, too. You have his sensitivity, Jim. He asked me a whole bunch of questions about the circumstances surrounding your decision, and when I was done answering them (hours later!), he nodded. I asked him if he was angry with you and he said no, that he understood exactly what had happened. There was this look in his blue eyes, a faraway look, Jim. I know your father was a marine in World War II, and I wonder if some terrible atrocity happened to him, too, and that's why he understands your situation. I'm sure you two will have a lot to talk about when you come home.

I'm going to be sending you a big "care package" of material—something to keep your mind busy while your body's imprisoned, so to speak. If you want to sign up for a correspondence course, let me know, and I'll help you.

I'm counting the days until you get home. And I'll be waiting for you. This isn't goodbye. You're not getting rid of me, Jim McKenzie. There's so much I'd like to say, but knowing my letters are going to be read by a stranger before they reach you stops me from being too private. I hope you

understand. I pray for you every night, and I
know your parents do, too. My love to you.

Alex

Jim sat in his cell, the darkness chased away by
lights in the aisle outside the bars. Alex's letter sent an
incredible wave of joy through him. Spread across his
thin mattress was a heap of material, mostly college-
related. His hands shook as he folded the pale pink
stationery. Alex had thoughtfully daubed a bit of
perfume on each page, and compared to the sweaty,
stale air of the jail, the scent was heavenly.

His cellmate, an army private who had gone AWOL,
was asleep in the upper bunk. Frowning, Jim looked
at the date of Alex's letter: mid-June. It was already
mid-July. Were they holding up his mail? Probably, as
part of the subtle and not-so-subtle punishment they
meted out to him on a daily basis. He'd read Alex's
letter so many times that the edges of the paper were
sweat-stained and dog-eared.

He appreciated the box of information she'd sent.
It sure beat sitting around at night with nothing to do.
Jim could stand anything except inactivity. Working
hard made the daytime hours go by rapidly, but when
evening fell, he felt like a trapped animal wanting to
howl out his pain at being imprisoned. Night was
when the full weight of his tortured conscience came
to life, when he felt deeply about Kim's death. Night
was something he dreaded even more than the regular
harassment from the guards.

In Alex's box were not only several college cata-
logs, but paper, envelopes and stamps so that he would

write back to her. His mouth curved into a slight smile. He knew the brig guards would already have gone through the contents thoroughly. Alex had baked a tin of cookies and the tin was there, but all that was in it were a few crumbs as a blatant reminder of who was in control.

Anger threaded through Jim, but he understood the mentality of the brig guards: they hated the prisoners because in some way, each had broken strict military rules, labeling them misfits. And in the Marine Corps, especially, there was no place for a misfit. The cookie tin was painted with bright spring flowers, and Jim looked at it a long time before setting it aside. There were newspaper and magazine articles about himself and Alex. Those he read with hungry intensity. One newspaper quoted Alex's father as saying that Jim deserved a firing squad, not publicity, for what he'd done. Silently, Jim agreed that he deserved it—but for killing Kim, not for refusing to carry out a superior officer's order to pick up a rifle and kill.

What was Alex really going through with her father? Jim wondered. He laid the items aside and thought again about her letter. It was so frustrating that she couldn't write how she truly felt about many things, understanding that censors read his mail. He dug deeper into the box. There were several hardbound books by Carl G. Jung, a psychiatric pioneer and student of Freud. Alex had penned on the outside of the first volume:

Jim, start reading these cover to cover! I love Jung, and I love his understanding of the human psyche. I found myself in these volumes as I read them last year, and wanted to share them with you. See if you find yourself!

"Hey, McKenzie."

Jim saw Private First Class Wood, an army guard, outside his cell. "Yes?"

Wood grinned and held up a colored photograph. "Your girl sent this, but we didn't think you deserved to keep it."

Frowning, Jim realized Alex had sent a small color photo of herself. He could barely make it out in the dim light. "That belongs to me."

Wood's smile broadened as he held up the photo. "Like hell it does. You know, those cookies she made for you were real good. Peanut butter. Too bad you didn't deserve them, either. As for this picture...well..." He slowly tore it in two, letting the pieces flutter to the concrete floor.

It took everything Jim had not to leap off the bunk and make a grab for Wood. But he knew better. Ever since he'd gotten to Long Binh, they'd been pushing him to blow up. They wanted to find any excuse to take him into solitary, where they'd beat the hell out of him with rubber hoses. Rubber didn't leave as many bruises as wooden billy clubs. Jim had seen other prisoners goaded beyond their limits, and the resulting beatings they took at the hands of the brig guards. His mouth compressed as Wood stood belligerently, waiting for Jim to lose control.

Jim kept his roiling emotions in tight check, forcing himself to return to the box before him and say nothing. If he said one word, he knew Wood could drag him out of the cell and force hours of calisthenics on him at the very least. At worst, Wood had his buddies waiting outside the outer door, salivating to give Jim a beating.

"What this girl sees in you is beyond us," Wood shouted, and he took the heel of his boot and ground it into the torn photo lying on the deck.

Clenching his teeth, Jim ignored the brig guard. Under his anger, he realized with startling clarity that the picture of Alex he held in his heart could never be taken from him. His dreams about her were beautiful and poignant. They were only dreams, but they were important to keeping his sanity in this insane environment.

July 15, 1965

Dear Alex,

Your box arrived and it was a real surprise—but a nice one. Your letter meant a lot to me. Thanks for the cookies and the photograph. I've looked through the correspondence courses you sent along and have made a choice: sociology looks good to me. And those books by Jung are real interesting. I think I'll read the one on dreams first, as I have a lot of those.

I'm filling out the correspondence-course forms in hope that you can help me get started. Ask my folks for the money you'll need—I had an allotment sent home monthly since I've been in Nam. The money's in a special bank account, and I know my ma can help you with that.

I'm doing fine. The leg is pretty much healed up now, and the cast comes off next week. I get a lot of physical exercise, which I don't mind, and it helps the hours go by. I hope your father realizes the bravery of his daughter, her goodness, her courage and the hope she gives to others.

Your letters are sunlight to me. The picture I hold of you in my heart is even more important than the photo you sent. I'll bet you're looking forward to ending summer classes so you can graduate this September. I wish I could be there to see it all.

I'll look forward to hearing from the college on this sociology correspondence course. I owe you so much, Alex, I don't know how I'll ever repay you, gal.

Your friend, Jim McKenzie

August 20, 1965

Dear Jim,

I guess our mail is having trouble reaching us. I just got your July letter. That bothers me. I'm going to make some inquiries to see if our lines of communication can't be straightened out.

I've already contacted the college for you, and driven over to see your folks again. I shared the letters from you with them, and they were beside themselves. Your mother withdrew the money from your savings, and the correspondence course is paid for. You should be receiving the first lesson shortly. If you don't, let me know.

I had a wonderful time with your folks! I spent the weekend with them, and guess what? They let me have your bedroom! I didn't realize you slept in the attic! Your mother was so emotional when I came. She told me that I was more like a daughter than an "outsider"—you know, one of those city folk from some other state! She's kept your room exactly as you left it. I loved seeing the photo of you in your marine uniform. It's proudly displayed on the wall of their living room.

Your mother showed me all the wonderful animals that you've carved since you were a kid. I never knew you were such an artist! She has them all up on a small walnut shelf in your bedroom, and dusts them weekly. She told me the stories behind each of the carved animals, and they made me cry. But they were tears of happiness, not sadness, Jim. To be able to touch the smooth wood, to run my fingers along that wonderfully sleek surface told me much about you, your discipline, your attention to detail, and the care you take with all things in your life. My favorite is the turtle. Ma, as she insists I call her, told me that you saved a box turtle from being killed by rescuing it off the highway after it had been struck. She said the turtle, who you called Priscilla, had her shell cracked. Ma said you taped up Prissy's shell, kept her in a nice box with dry grass and hand fed her until she got well. I cried.

Your father is so shy... he just sort of hangs back watching Ma and me. But I can tell he's glad

I came. Last night after dinner, he took me into their bedroom and showed me his old trunk. We must have sat in there looking over the contents for three hours, Jim. He told me about his six years as a marine and showed me his uniforms. How proud he is of them, and well he should be. Probably the most touching was when he let me hold the silver star he'd earned and given to you. When he told me how he'd earned it, I cried for him, for you, myself and all the people who have to fight wars. Now I know where you got your bravery. He's also proud of the silver star *you* earned last year. So am I.

Your ma is swearing to make me a good Missouri hill cook! She's been drilling me on slang, and giving me recipes like blue john and corn pone, showing me the difference between good pork bacon and fat back. I'm learning how to make the most wonderful-tasting corn bread in the world! I brought the recipe back to my mother. I'm sure she'll love it, too.

I was sad to leave your folks, but had to get home. I'll graduate from college in just two more weeks and become an RN. My folks will come to the ceremony. My father grumps that I should think about getting a commission and joining the navy or air force, but I told him no. I only wish you could be here to see me graduate.

I've sent my résumé to a VA hospital in Portland, Oregon, so keep your fingers crossed for me! I should hear shortly, Mrs. Riddell said. speaking of her, we finished off my battle-fatigue questionnaire. I hope to pursue the project at my new job. She feels it's a worthwhile project, and so do I. And she pointed out to me that my understanding of what war can do is a plus to the patients I'll care for. She's right. What's the old adage: It Takes One to Know One?

My shoulder is doing really well. I've got about ninety-five percent mobility back now, and all that's left is a pink scar. It gets cranky during damp weather, particularly just before a rainstorm. Maybe I'll be a barometer. Ha ha.

Things are settling down with my father. He's speaking to me again, albeit stiffly. At least we're talking. Mother says he's got his mind on too many other things at the Hill to stay angry at me much longer. Someday, I hope I can sit down and talk quietly and without anger to him about the choices I've made. I wish Father could be more like you—easy to talk to. You never lose your temper, and I'm in awe of that ability.

Oh, I'm sending over a tin of *homemade* Missouri corn bread from your mother's recipe. It's a little slice of home, and I know you'll appreciate it. You are always in my dreams, Jim, and my heart. Time hasn't dulled my feelings for you; it's only made them stronger. I hope it's the same for you.

With love, Alex

September 3, 1965

Dear Alex,

I sure got your last letter in a hurry. Congratulations on your graduation! I hope by the time my letter reaches you, you've got that job you want in Portland. Reading your letter was like being home. I wish I'd been there to hold you when you cried over Prissy's story, or when my pa opened up his trunk and shared it with you. I hope you know he considers you real special. I didn't get to see anything in that trunk until I told him I wanted to join up with the marines. You're special, Alexandra Vance. Very special in my eyes and heart.

The corn bread arrived. Thank you. I've received the first lesson of my correspondence course. The more I think about it, I believe sociology's a good place for me to start. I've always been interested in what makes people tick.

My leg is fine now, and I'm out doing my duty a full ten or twelve hours a day along with everyone else. By the time I get back to my cell, I'm pretty tired. We don't get much word about what's going on out in the real world, or even here in Nam. I appreciate the magazines and newspapers you're sending. A lot of times I fall asleep halfway through an article, but that's okay.

I know that your being with Ma is helping her a lot through this period. I'm sure you're sunlight to them, like you are to me. My pa isn't one to say much, he just watches and studies people from a distance. He's a pretty shy man, and I guess I'm a lot like him in that way. In my heart, I know your being there for both of them has eased their pain over what I've gotten myself into. I owe you so much, gal. Please keep writing.

Your friend, Jim McKenzie

Alex reread Jim's letter for the sixth time, trying to ferret out the true meaning of his words—reading between the lines, as Matt Breckenridge had warned she'd have to do. The mild October breeze flowed through her newly rented home in Portland, Oregon. The VA hospital had eagerly hired her, and within two weeks Alex had moved from one coast to the other. Never had she been happier—or more lonely. This was the first time in her life she was without the proximity of her family. Most of all, she missed quiet talks with her understanding mother. Going to work at the VA hospital was helping her pass the time until Jim came home. Alex frowned. What had happened to the other letters she'd sent? Since August, she had sent five letters and none of them had garnered responses. Was Jim not getting them? Was he not answering them? Or were they holding up his mail back to her?

Frustrated, Alex poured herself a glass of iced tea and leaned against the kitchen counter. The linoleum felt cool beneath her bare feet. She worried for Jim, for the hard labor he was obviously doing. More importantly, he'd asked her to keep writing to him, as if he'd finally accepted that she wasn't going to abandon him—no matter what. Still, he hadn't ever signed a letter "love," as she did.

Chewing her lower lip, Alex tried to grapple with her feelings. She knew she loved Jim. But he'd never said he loved her. Was it really a one-way street? Alex moved slowly through the kitchen and back into the small living room. She sat down on the couch and curled her legs beneath her.

Jim would be released from Long Binh in late November, according to a recent letter from Lieutenant Breckenridge. He hadn't known the exact date, but said Jim would more than likely write and let her know. Would Jim come and see her? Would he say goodbye to her in one of his letters before he left Vietnam? Everything was so tenuous, and disappointment thrummed through Alex. She couldn't pose such questions to Jim via letters, because of the censors. Alex would just have to wait, the hardest thing in the world for her to do. November couldn't come too soon.

Chapter Ten

"Hey!" Gary called from his bed, "Tomorrow's Thanksgiving, Miss Vance. Are you gonna be here?"

Alex stood at the locked doors to the psychiatric ward of the VA hospital where she worked. She smiled at Gary, a twenty-year-old marine who had "gone crazy" over in Vietnam, had summarily been given a medical discharge and had found his way here for help. He sat in his light blue pajamas, painfully thin, his dark eyes burning with the horror he still carried within him.

"You bet, Gary."

He clapped his hands like a delighted child. "Groovy!" Then he turned and looked down the long rectangular room filled with patients and beds. "Hey, guys! Miss Vance is too gonna be here!"

Sporadic clapping, hooting, hollering and whistles started, and Alex lifted her hand in farewell to her patients, these men that she had come to love with a fierce loyalty. John Sheldrick, one of the hospital orderlies, let her out, promptly locking the door behind her again.

"You're getting out of here late, Alex," he noted, looking at his watch.

"I know."

"Is it because of that newby? Grant?"

She picked up her dark brown wool coat and shrugged it over her white uniform. "Yes. How did you know?"

John smiled and shrugged. "I know your interest in that combat-symptom project of yours. Did he answer all the questions you asked him?"

"All of them," Alex said, pleased. John was a big man in his mid-forties, an ex-army sergeant who had put in twenty years but couldn't leave the realm of military life. "Even you said the questionnaire had merit. Just for your information, Chuck Grant fits the definition for the fatigue syndrome. Satisfied?"

John sank into the squeaky chair, the lights low because it was nearly 10:00 p.m. "Yup," he said thoughtfully. "You bring an umbrella? It's raining out there."

"Again?" Alex muttered. She slung her black leather purse over her arm and hunted in a large can behind the desk for her red umbrella. "I never realized Portland had so much rain."

"It's late fall. What do you expect? Can't snow here, so it's gotta do something depressing."

She smiled. "I suppose you're right."

"Hey, what about McKenzie? Ain't he supposed to be coming home from Nam soon?"

Alex straightened and unsnapped the loop around the umbrella. Her heart raced. Since she'd come to the VA hospital on the outskirts of Portland, John had become her friend and confidant. He knew about Jim and his prison term.

"I—I don't know, John."

"He was getting out this month?"

"Yes." Alex frowned. "The last I heard from Jim was September. I've continued sending letters, but he hasn't answered them." Alex's throat ached with the tension of unshed tears. She had tried to find out Jim's release date, but had repeatedly been stymied by military bureaucracy. She had no idea if Jim was coming home, or if he would visit her once he was released.

Scratching his thinning black hair, John muttered, "If I know those brig goons, they probably confiscated your letters before Jim got them." Then he grinned, his green eyes lighting up. "Hey, now don't you lose that pretty smile of yours. These guys wait each afternoon until you come on shift just to see your smile. You're their sunshine, you know. And their favorite nurse."

Sunshine. Jim's word for her. Alex rallied and nodded. "I hope he knows I love him, John. With or without the letters reaching him."

"If he don't by now, he don't deserve you."

Alex went over to give John a hug. "You're good for *my* morale, John."

"Hey," he chided her, "now don't you give up on this McKenzie." He thumped his chest. "I got a feeling in here about him. From what you've told me, he's a good man in a bad situation. You deserve each other. Just don't give up hope."

"I wrote his parents a letter last week," Alex said. "I told them to tell Jim I wanted to see him, that I loved him." Did he love her? Alex gnawed on her lower lip, close to tears.

"So you gonna spend your hard-earned day off celebrating Thanksgiving with the guys in here? It's all they've talked about for a week. Are you really gonna eat dinner with them?"

"Yes. I promised I'd bake them some homemade corn bread and pumpkin pies." Alex glanced at her watch. "Gosh, I've got to get going! I've got four pies to make tonight before I go to bed."

"I hope those bastards know how lucky they are to have you as their nurse. Maybe I'll get a piece of one of those pies, too? I have to work tomorrow, Alex."

"Of course you will, John! Bye," she called, quickly walking down the empty hall. The walls were painted light green, shadowy now that most of the lights were turned out.

In the huge, silent asphalt parking lot, rain fell at a light, steady rate. The streetlights helped her locate her blue station wagon, her first purchase since having a job of her own. The depressing weather settled in on Alex as she unlocked the car door and slid onto the seat. She tried not to think about Jim.

As Alex drove to her rented house not far from the hospital, her heart began to ache in earnest. Was Jim home yet? Her cold fingers gripped the steering wheel even more firmly as she drove slowly through the suburban streets of Portland. Lights reflected off the wet pavement, and darkness hovered.

Pulling into the concrete driveway of her small, one-story home, Alex stopped and climbed out of the car. She hurried up the sidewalk and steps. Inside, her cat, Thomasina, greeted her.

"Hi, Tommy," Alex said as she shut the door. The cat meowed a welcome from where she sat. Alex couldn't stand living completely alone and had been delighted when Thomasina had found her way to the front porch one stormy night in October. The black-and-gray striped cat with huge yellow eyes had been a permanent fixture since that night.

Hurrying to her bedroom, Alex got out of her white nursing uniform and pulled on a long-sleeved white blouse, a pair of jeans and a red cardigan. It was cool in the house, and Alex turned up the thermostat before she went to the kitchen. Pies had to be made. Four of them! Alex knew that her fifteen patients were starving for a touch of home life. They had no family who would come to visit over the special holiday.

Thomasina leaped up onto one of the four kitchen chairs surrounding a round table covered with a pink linen tablecloth. Alex had planned for the pies and had made the crusts for them last week. All she had to do now was make the pumpkin filling. She turned on the radio that sat atop the refrigerator and hummed along with the soft FM music as she worked at the kitchen counter.

By eleven, Alex sat relaxing at the table, her pies in the oven, baking. Thomasina slept on the chair next to her, and Alex had rewarded herself with a well-deserved cup of tea. With any luck, she'd be in bed by midnight.

The doorbell rang.

Frowning, Alex sat up. So did Thomasina.

"I wonder who that is," she said to the cat.

Thomasina stared at her, unblinking.

Walking through the darkened living room, Alex switched on a lamp near the flowery print couch. There was no window in the door, so she couldn't tell who it might be. Keeping the guard chain on, Alex cautiously opened the door.

"Alex?"

A gasp escaped her. "Jim!"

He stood uncertainly, dressed in civilian clothes and a dark blue raincoat. "Hi. I know it's late, but—"

"Just a minute..." Shakily, Alex took the chain off the door. Her heart pounding triple time, she pulled the door open. Her eyes went wide as she looked up into Jim's shadowed features, glistening with rain. Anguish seared Alex and her breath caught in her throat. Jim looked gaunt, and she could see the unsureness in his eyes. A slight smile barely tipped the corners of his mouth.

"Come in," she whispered unsteadily, catching his hand and pulling him into the carpeted foyer. Shutting the door, Alex stood back, shocked. The light on Jim's face showed unbearable tension in his features. His dark hair was wet and small rivulets of water ran down his neck, soaking into his plaid shirt. What hurt the most was a new scar that ran from his temple to his jaw. Alex knew immediately that he'd been badly beaten in Long Binh. Tears came to her eyes, but she fought them back.

"I—I didn't know if you'd come," she whispered lamely. "I hadn't heard from you for so long...."

"I'm sorry, Alex. I tried to call." Jim stood uncertainly in the unfamiliar but cozy surroundings of Alex's home. He saw her soft, dove gray eyes grow large with pain. As if realizing Alex was staring at his recently healed injury, he reached up and self-consciously touched the scar on the side of his face.

"I'm so happy to see you," she quavered.

"I got Stateside this morning—"

"Please, take off that coat. You're wet." He was shivering, and when Alex touched the coat, she realized the material was soaked all the way through. "How long have you been out in this rain?"

Jim unbuttoned the coat. "An hour...maybe a little longer. I caught the bus from San Francisco to Portland, then walked over here from the station."

"My God, that's six miles away. Why didn't you call from the bus terminal?"

"I did, but you weren't home."

Alex rolled her eyes. "I took two shifts today to give my friend Gail a chance to go home for the holidays." It was on the tip of her tongue to ask why he hadn't gotten a cab, but Alex remembered Jim had little money. All of his meager private's pay was going into his savings account in Missouri. She took the coat and quickly carried it to the laundry room.

Returning, Alex saw that Jim was hesitantly looking around. But the moment he heard her approach, his gaze settled on her. She slowed as she approached, wanting so badly to throw her arms around him and hold him . . . simply hold him. His eyes were shadowy with exhaustion, and there were rings under them. But the moment he gave her that easy, boyish smile, all of Alex's fears melted away.

"Oh, Jim!" She opened her arms and pressed herself to him.

Jim groaned at the unexpected gift of Alex in his arms. All he could do was hold her, feel her breathing against him, inhale her feminine scent and bury his face in her luxurious sable hair, now shoulder length.

"I thought—I thought maybe you didn't want to see me again," he rasped, his eyes tightly shut, savoring Alex against him.

"No . . . no, I do." Alex sobbed. "You never received my letters?"

Jim slowly eased his embrace and looked down at her suffering features. Gently, he caressed Alex's flaming cheek. The tears in her eyes reminded him of beautiful diamonds. "The last one I got was dated September."

Alex shut her eyes tightly. "Those bastards! I hate them! I hate what they've done to you—to us!" She opened her eyes and drowned in his sad azure gaze. "Jim, I sent you a letter every week or so."

Anger surged through Jim, and he steadied his grip around Alex. "I never got them."

Alex dashed away her tears. "You look so tired." She tried not to stare at the fresh, terrible-looking scar.

It showed the marks of at least twenty stitches. Inwardly, Alex shuddered, afraid to know how Jim had gotten it and how much he must have suffered after receiving it.

He tested the air with his nose. "Right now, gal, I could stand a little food in this shrunken belly of mine, and a good cup of hot coffee. I haven't eaten since this mornin'. Whatever you're baking sure smells good."

Alex rallied beneath his husky tone. "You came to the right place, then. Come on, Jim McKenzie. I intend to stuff you with home-cooked food until you burst."

Jim's mouth stretched tiredly, and he held Alex's small hand as he followed her into the kitchen. He sat down at the table, a contentment flowing through him that he'd never dreamed of feeling. Alex was wearing a red-and-white checked apron, her lovely hair mussed and framing her flushed features. A cat came over and jumped onto his lap, purring madly. He gently stroked the affectionate feline.

"I wasn't even sure you'd be home. Since I hadn't gotten you on the phone, I thought you might have gone home to see your folks over Thanksgiving."

Alex shook her head and placed a salad in front of him. "No, I wanted to be here with my patients." She took Thomasina and placed her on the floor. "They don't have anyone nearby," she explained as she brought salad dressing from the refrigerator.

"Just like you," Jim said. He was starving, and said nothing more as he dug into the salad of Bibb lettuce, carrots, tomatoes and bits of purple cabbage. The pleasant clink of kitchen pots and pans were like music to him. In no time, Alex had cooked him pork chops, steamed some frozen corn and taken some previously baked potatoes and fried them up as well. It was a feast to Jim. Within half an hour, he was stuffed like the proverbial turkey.

Alex took the four pumpkin pies from the oven and set them on the counter to cool. She saw the color coming back to Jim's pale face, his eyes look more alert. Taking a seat across from him as he finished some chocolate cake, she sat quietly, just watching him.

"You're really here," she said finally, awe in her voice.

Jim lifted his head. He wiped his mouth with the pink linen napkin and set it aside. "I feel like I'm in a dream, too."

"A beautiful dream," Alex whispered shyly.

"I don't ever want to wake up."

She didn't either. The darkness beneath his eyes had increased. "You need to sleep."

"Yeah..." Jim frowned. "Look, I don't want to impose on you, Alex—"

"The couch turns into a bed. You could stay here," Alex offered quickly.

Relief flowed through him. "I'll take you up on your kindness. To tell you the truth, I'm short on money. I've got to get to a Western Union station tomorrow, wire my folks for some money and let them know I arrived safely Stateside."

"Of course." Alex stood. "Let me make your bed up. Could you use a hot shower?"

"How about a hot bath? I haven't had one since...well, a long time ago. I'd give almost anything to just sit and soak in some hot water."

She smiled gently. "Come on, I'll show you where the bathroom's located and get you a towel and washcloth."

Jim got up and followed her. His throat constricted with emotions that were in utter chaos. To come out of the damp, smelly cell where he'd been under the brutal attention of the brig guards for four months into this clean, lovely home was too much to comprehend. Jim was sure he was experiencing some kind of culture shock. Everything about Alex's home was clean, the odors tantalizing, and the colors soft, like her.

By the time Alex had made the couch into a bed, Jim appeared in the living-room doorway. Alex had loaned him her huge, oversize blue terry-cloth bathrobe, and although it barely fit, he didn't mind. He sure didn't want to put his damp clothes back on. Alex put an extra blanket at the bottom of the bed, in case he got cold.

"Come on, you look like you're going to keel over, Jim."

"The bed does look good," he agreed. Exhaustion was lapping at all his senses, and he heard himself slurring his words. Dropping his shoes and socks nearby, he sat down on the edge of the bed. He patted the mattress. "Feels good, too."

Alex moved to the doorway. "Sleep as long as you want. I'll probably be up around eight, and I've got the afternoon shift at the hospital."

"What time do you get off?"

"Nine p.m."

Jim nodded. "Good."

"Why?"

"No reason. The way I'm feeling, I'll probably sleep all night and most of tomorrow."

Alex wanted to kiss him, but she fought herself. Although he had held her tightly in his arms, he hadn't kissed her, hadn't said he loved her. Filled with uncertainty, Alex whispered, "Good night, Jim."

"Good night, gal."

The room grew quiet after Alex left. Soon, the kitchen light switched off and Jim shrugged out of the robe. What little money he'd had was already spent. The clothes on his back had been purchased in Saigon before he'd boarded the freedom bird for home— and for a new life.

Just the act of lying on a soft mattress, with clean white sheets, was amazing. His brain was fogged with weariness as he shaped the pillow with his long, spare fingers and closed his eyes. *Alex.* He was here, with her. At her home. He'd found her, and she'd welcomed him. Did she love him? Was there something left of their long-ago experience on which to build? Everything was so uncertain. Jim sighed raggedly, spiraling into a dark, dreamless sleep—his first in four months.

Alex awoke at eight in a euphoria of happiness. As she lay in her room, the morning sun peeking in through the white curtains at the window, she suddenly remembered that Jim was here. Sitting up, her flannel granny gown rumpled, Alex pushed her hair out of her eyes. *Jim was here.*

Some of her happiness ebbed as she continued waking up. What she wanted was Jim in her bed—with her. The need to love him, to physically bond with him, was eating away at Alex. As she got up, took a hot shower and changed into dark green slacks and an ivory sweater, she felt giddy and nervous. Was he awake yet? She wondered how he'd slept last night— if he'd had any nightmares.

Tiptoeing to the living room, Alex felt her nervousness recede. Jim lay on his left side, sleeping deeply, the blankets pooled around his waist. Thomasina lay in his arms, and a smile tugged at Alex's mouth as the cat blinked awake and stared across the room toward her.

Alex absorbed Jim's sleeping features. His hair was cut very short, and even in the gloom of the living room, Alex could still see the welt of that evil scar. What had happened? She tucked her lower lip between her teeth, feeling pain. His pain. Jim's mouth was slightly parted, the tension he'd carried the night before gone. Even the darkness beneath his long, spiky lashes had nearly disappeared. He was sleeping well, his darkly haired chest rising and falling slowly.

A newfound yearning cascaded through Alex. She carefully made her way out to the kitchen. The pies for her patients would have to be packed and the corn bread, baked last week, taken from the freezer. She needed to be at the hospital by eleven so she'd have time to make sure the preparations for Thanksgiving dinner went just right. Making a pot of coffee as quietly as she could, Alex penned Jim a note and laid it nearby.

After feeding Thomasina, Alex puttered quietly around the house and did a load of laundry. Eleven o'clock approached and Alex didn't want to go. She wanted to stay and watch Jim awaken, to talk to him and spend hours catching up on his life. She had so many questions, so many blank spots that needed to be filled in. As she placed the pies in the car, Alex knew that they'd have that time. Still, this was one day—even though it was special to her patients—that she wanted to pass quickly. By nine-thirty tonight she'd be home. *Home.* And Jim would be waiting for her. As Alex backed the car out of the driveway, she felt as if her life was beginning all over again, excitement and fear vying for attention within her.

Alex was about to open her front door when Jim opened it for her. She smiled up at him. He was clean shaven, wearing the clothes she'd washed for him that morning. Shadows no longer lurked beneath his eyes, and there was a ruddiness to his complexion and a twinkle in his cobalt eyes.

"Hi!"

Jim smiled. "Hi yourself, gal."

Alex walked into the foyer and shed her coat. Jim took it and hung it up in the hall closet.

"This is the first time I've seen you in a nurse's uniform," he teased. Catching her hand, he pulled her to a stop. "Hold on, let me take a good look at you. Last night, I wasn't all here."

Blushing furiously, Alex stood still beneath his intense inspection. Touching her hair nervously, she muttered, "I look a mess right now—"

"No," Jim said, "you look purty as ever. You always will to me, Alex." His fingers tightened around hers as he looked deeply into her lovely gray eyes. There was such beauty to her red lips and the way they parted beneath his hungry inspection. Jim hotly recalled his kissing Alex so long ago. That one exquisite moment they'd shared had never left him, no matter how bad things had gotten.

Alex stood very still, her senses spinning. The look in Jim's eyes was making her shaky inside. "I—I'm scared," she whispered.

He managed a one-cornered smile. "So am I, gal. I'm scared of myself, of the feelings I have for you. It's been so long, Alex, so long without you...."

She swallowed hard and nodded. Jim was so close. Just two steps and she would be in his arms. But did he love her? What was left between them? "I'm afraid of myself, of my feelings, too, if it makes you feel any better." She laughed nervously.

Jim released her hand, although he didn't want to. "I have a proposal for you, Alex. It's something... well, something I dreamed about while I was in Long Binh. Maybe it's a crazy dream, an impossible one...."

"What is it?" She held her breath.

Jim shrugged. "I thought...well...that is, I'd like you to take some time off to be with me. I know this is sudden and unexpected. When I didn't receive any more mail from you, I was afraid to propose the idea in a letter to you." He held her lustrous gaze. "We need time for ourselves, Alex. I guess that's what I'm saying. I wired my folks this afternoon, and they sent me the money."

She looked down at the carpet. "My supervisor knew you were coming home." Alex took in a ragged breath. "I was hoping you'd ask. I took the week off, Jim, just in case you showed up here."

"I'm glad you did, gal," he whispered huskily. Reaching out, he caressed Alex's cheek, her skin velvety beneath his touch.

Braving her fear, Alex looked up as he cupped her cheek with his long, scarred fingers. "Jim, I never stopped loving you. Not ever. You weren't some passing fancy to me. And it wasn't because of what happened in Vietnam, either."

Aching to take her, to love her, Jim nodded, the words stuck in his throat in a big lump. Taking a step closer, he allowed his hand to fall on her small shoulder. "You're so brave," he told her unsteadily, "so brave. I hope, Alex, I can match your courage. Maybe this next week will tell us what we both need to know."

Alex shut her eyes. She loved him so fiercely, unequivocally, that there was only one thing that she wanted from him: his love in return. "I'll take the time off, Jim," she heard herself say, her voice sounding hollow with fear.

Chapter Eleven

"First things first," Jim told Alex as he walked to the kitchen with her. When he saw the delight in her eyes, he smiled down at her. "A gentleman always courts a lady proper. Just because we got off on the wrong foot doesn't mean we can't right things now. I'd like to take you out to dinner."

Heat raced up Alex's cheeks, and she felt shaky inside once again. The words "court you proper" hung gently before her, and she couldn't overcome her own fear to ask him what he meant. So often, she'd found out in the past, Missouri hill slang meant something entirely different from what she thought.

"Dessert?"

His smile deepened. "It's Thanksgiving. I know you've already eaten, but I haven't. And no one should be alone on a holiday like this." He grazed her flaming cheek with his fingers. "Besides, I'm thankful for so many things. For you, for your loyalty... You never gave up on me, Alex. I owe you more than I can ever repay."

She swallowed, hurt jagging through her. Alex didn't want to be paid back. Was this what the dinner proposal was about? Repayment for her support during some of the darkest hours of his life? "You don't have any obligations to me," she managed in a hoarse tone. "None. I did what I did because of how I feel about you, Jim."

"I'm not asking you on this date out of obligation. It's important that we do things right," Jim said calmly, although every bit of his being was aching to lean down and kiss her ripe, red lips. "Will you humor this guy from Missouri and go out with him? Our first official date?"

"I'd love nothing better than to be with you."

Jim stood and forced himself to place his hands in the pockets of his brown slacks. Alex wore an uncertain expression on her face, and Jim didn't know how to interpret it. Perhaps she was ashamed to be seen in public with him—because of his past, a past that would live with him forever.

"Sure?"

"Positive. Do you have a place picked out?"

"No. I figured you knew Portland well enough to suggest a nice restaurant." He glanced down at his large feet encased in brown leather loafers. "I'm afraid I can't dance worth nothing, gal."

"I'm not much on dancing, either, if the truth be known. It's a holiday and late, but I think The Top

Shelf is open. It's not too far from here. They even serve steaks.''

''I'd give my right arm for a good steak,'' Jim said fervently. He couldn't recall when he'd had a decent meal except for last night. The food at Long Binh had been minimal and poorly prepared.

With a laugh, Alex nodded. ''Let me take a quick shower and change into something more appropriate than this uniform.''

Jim couldn't take his eyes off Alex as they sat in a secluded black-leather booth at the elegant restaurant. The interior of The Top Shelf was dimly lit and very private, the music soft and unobtrusive. It matched Jim's feelings: he needed privacy, to be alone to speak at length with Alex about so many things of importance.

Everything paled in comparison to Alex. She wore a lavender dress with a square neck and an Empire waistline. The light wool gown was long-sleeved, with seven tiny pearl buttons running up each sleeve. Jim thought she looked like a fairy-tale princess come to life. Her hair, shining with highlights beneath the lamps, was tucked tastefully into a French twist, the feathery bangs across her brow only making her more exquisitely feminine. The pearl necklace and pearl earrings emphasized her flushed features.

''I feel like a hog in a pigsty compared to how purty you look, Alex.'' Jim had gone out that afternoon to a shopping center and bought a pair of navy slacks and a tan corduroy sports coat. The white cotton dress shirt fit him poorly, because of his weight loss. He'd had to buy the right size for his long arms, so the fabric was wrinkled, particularly across his chest. The tie, a brown-and-blue paisley, matched his outfit, he supposed. He'd never been good at dressing up. Suits and ties hadn't been part of his life in Missouri. The Marine Corps had taught him how to properly knot a tie, and he'd gotten his too tight tonight because of his nervousness about his date with Alex. Jim dug a finger into the collar around his throat and tugged at it, trying to loosen the strangling tie.

"You don't look like a pig in a sty," Alex said and slid her hand into his. Jim's fingers were long and firm around her own. "To me, you look like a handsome prince come to take me to dinner."

Pleasantly surprised, Jim smiled. "I'm afraid Ma didn't know a lot about table manners and all. She did the best she could with the likes of me." Jim had been aghast at first, worried by the array of silverware when they were ushered to their table. "One thing I remember. Ma always said to start from the outside and work in."

"Your mother was right," Alex said. In the low lights, Jim looked handsome in a harsh way. Like the patients she cared for, he had a wariness deep in his blue eyes, and he kept glancing around, tense and outwardly jumpy. When a waiter had dropped a glass at the station, Jim had winced and broken into a light sweat. He'd eaten well, and they turned down dessert in favor of a cup of rich Brazilian coffee. The waiter had cleared away the dishes and they were able to sit and hold hands.

Jim met Alex's gaze. "I guess it's time for some serious talk," he began. "There's so much I've been wanting to say to you, but couldn't in my letters."

"You know, Lieutenant Breckenridge warned me that you wouldn't be able to say much, that I'd have to read between the lines."

Sadly, Jim nodded. "That's true, gal." He gently stroked her fingers, wondering in his heart what it would be like to have Alex touch him. Jim gently put those yearnings away. "You know the food you sent? The cookies? The corn bread?"

"Yes."

"The brig guards confiscated all of it, Alex. I never got any of it." He saw her features cloud first with sadness and then anger. "Worst of all," he admitted, "was that purty color photo you sent early on. I didn't get that, either." He didn't tell her the full truth of the situation, not wanting to unduly upset Alex. She didn't deserve to go through the array of emotions he'd had when the brig chaser, Wood, had destroyed the photo out of pure meanness.

"That's inhumane!"

"It's all right, gal," he soothed. "They couldn't take you away from me. You were here in my head, and here in my heart." With a shrug, Jim added, "I'm just glad it's over, that's all." He drew her hand to his lips and kissed it. Her skin was fragrant with a spicy perfume.

His words, his actions, melted away her anger and left her breathless. Alex saw the haunted quality in his eyes. "I like being held in your heart," she whispered. And then, very gently, she asked, "What was it really like for you in there, Jim?"

Jim wanted to shield her from the worst of his imprisonment. He wouldn't lie to Alex ever, but he just wouldn't tell her the worst of it. "I did a lot of hard, physical labor—anywhere from eight to twelve hours a day. We got three square meals—"

"Sure you did. Look at you—you're skin and bones!"

He grinned slightly. "You know how purty you look when you're madder than a wet hen?"

Alex felt some of her anger dissolve beneath his husky teasing. "You always had the ability to settle me down. I do have a bad temper, sometimes."

"Naw, you're just a gal who feels deeply about things. That's one of the many things I like about you, Alex. Don't ever change that."

Flooded with joy at his compliments, Alex wanted to get back to his time spent in the jail. "Your letters kept me going," she admitted.

"I kept all the ones I received from you, Alex." He stared at her long, work-worn fingers. "You have no idea how much your words kept *me* going. There were times . . . well, Long Binh was a nightmare. Sometimes, when I'd get lower than a snake's belly in a wheel rut, I'd reread your letters, and I could hang on. For a while I started to believe what the brig guards were hammering into me—that I was no good. And then, about halfway through my prison term, with your letters and your faith that I could be something better than I'd ever dreamed, I began to find a new kind of strength."

Jim's mouth lifted in a slight smile that was more a grimace. "I'd gotten beaten down, Alex, in an emotional sense. You were like a bright, clear light in my darkness. The correspondence course in sociology was a lifesaver. I began to see and understand people and their reactions differently than before. You helped me get my head above water and survive in that place."

Alex nodded and laid her hand over his. "Your letters began to sound stronger, more sure."

"Thanks to you."

"No," Alex countered with feeling, "you pulled yourself up by your own bootstraps, Jim. I could be there to suggest things, but you were the one who decided to put them into action."

"Well, I don't think I'd have made it through this last four months without you being there, Alex. I thought being a recon was hell at times, but I was wrong. Long Binh is truly hell on earth."

Alex could only sit there, feeling deeply for his painful admission. "What now, Jim? What are your plans?"

He held her luminous gray gaze. There was such depth of feeling in her eyes. All Jim wanted to do was bury himself in Alex's arms, wrap himself in her love. But that wouldn't be fair to her. They had to have time to get to know one another. "Most of what I do hinges on you, Alex."

"Me?" Her heart began to pound slowly.

"Yeah." Jim's grip on her hand tightened. "Since I have a bad conduct discharge, my GI benefits are cut off. If I go to college, it means getting a couple of jobs on the side to pay for books and tuition, plus finding a place to live. I can do all that. Any place I go to get a job will automatically ask me about my military enlistment. Once they find out I had a BCD, they won't hire me, so I'll have to go for labor kinds of jobs, instead.

"My dream at this point is to get a degree in psychology. I can see sociology's benefit, but like you, I'm interested in the mind and how it runs a person. I figure if I make outstanding grades, work hard, that four years will help erase my BCD up to a point." Jim shook his head. "That BCD will haunt me the rest of my life, Alex. It's liable to stop me from getting a really good job at some point in my future. I'll probably never make really good money, but that's not all that important to me. I have to be happy doing something that will help others."

"I understand," Alex whispered, fighting back her tears. "I like your plan. I think it will work."

"You do?"

"I know it will, Jim." She heard the hope in his voice, the need for someone to validate him. Jim was fragile in ways that Alex was only beginning to realize. Her love for him was overwhelming. Looking into his eyes, she sensed his tension, a taut nervousness that kept him tightly wound, and that haunted look that lingered. Alex tried to put herself in his shoes, coming out of a harrowing prison term and landing squarely back in civilization, with all its comforts and opportunities.

Alex took a deep breath and her hand tightened around his. "Jim, I know what I'm going to say isn't proper, and that society would frown on it. My parents won't like it either, but that's too bad.'' Alex gathered all her courage and held Jim's gaze. ''What would you think of moving to Portland and continuing your education at one of the colleges around here? That way, we could be close. We could pursue our relationship.''

Jim struggled to hold back the words *I love you,* which begged to be torn from him. ''I've thought about that,'' he whispered. ''But I worry for you, what your father might think.'' He flushed. ''I'd get my own place.'' Jim didn't want to ruin Alex's reputation—especially with her family.

''Of course. My father thinks my whole life is a mistake at this point, so it won't surprise him if you move to Portland, Jim.''

He hurt for Alex. ''I'm sorry, gal. You don't deserve that. I don't understand why your father doesn't see your kindness, your goodness.''

''Someday he might,'' Alex said, all at once emotionally gutted by their conversation. ''Right now, I live my own life on my own terms. He doesn't like it, but I'm not going to change. My mother understands and supports me completely.''

''Women are often the stronger ones,'' Jim said. ''And they have more insight. I hope someday to meet your mother.''

''I want you to, Jim.''

Squeezing her hand, he said, ''Let's go home.''

Alex agreed. The need to hold Jim, to touch him, kiss him, was nearly impossible to deal with in a public place. More than anything, Alex realized they simply needed each other, to explore what they did or didn't have. Her entire life felt as if it were on shifting, breakable eggshells.

At her house, Alex realized with a pang how exhausted Jim had become. There was so much he hadn't shared with her about Long Binh, but she was beginning to realize the toll it had taken on him in every way.

"I think we both need to go to bed and get a good night's sleep," she told him in the darkened living room.

Regret flowed through Jim, but he knew Alex was right. "As much as I want to keep talking, keep sharing, I'm plumb tuckered out, gal. I'm sorry."

She reached out and slid her hand along his arm. "Don't be. Remember? I'm the gal who's been taking care of returning Vietnam vets at the hospital. I'm trained to know when they've reached their personal limit." Risking everything, Alex stood on tiptoe and pressed a chaste kiss to his cheek where the scar lay. "We have a whole week, Jim. Good night...."

Afterward, Alex lay in her bed for a long time, sleep evading her. Normally, a hot shower, the fuzzy warmth of her long, flannel granny gown and her comfortable bed made her sleepy without fail. Not tonight. She lay on her back, her hands behind her head, and stared up at the ceiling. Street lamps took away the blackness, lighting her room in a gloomy gray. Glancing at the clock on the bedside table, Alex moved restlessly. It was two in the morning. Her covers were in tangles from her tossing and turning.

Finally, disgusted with the raw emotions that refused to be laid to rest, Alex got up. Her feet brushed the cool wooden floor, and she sat, feeling the mass of emotions within her. The need to love Jim, to reach out and heal him with her love, would no longer remain silent or under her control. Rubbing her face, Alex didn't know what to do. It was wrong to sleep with a man, any man, before marriage. Virginity was something valued, and up until now she had wanted to save herself for her husband.

Miserably, Alex looked around her room, at the frilly, pale pink curtains, the wallpaper with its tiny rosebud pattern. She had never felt more unhappy, or more torn. The door to her bedroom was open a crack so that Thomasina, who usually slept at the end of her bed, could come and go as she pleased. With a slight, pained smile, Alex realized that Thomasina had gone out to be with Jim, to sleep on his bed. The cat was lucky, Alex thought, that she didn't have social pressures to concern her.

Clenching her small fists, Alex remained in a quandary. Just as she got to her feet to retrieve her blue flannel robe from the bottom of her bed, she heard Jim scream.

Freezing, Alex heard him scream again. The sound, a horrible cry from the depths of a person trapped in hell, shattered the night's silence. Instantly, Alex ran out the door, down the hall and to the living room.

"Jim!" She found him sitting up, his hands pressed against his face, sobbing. "Oh, no..." Alex moved to his side. His upper body was naked and bathed in a sheen of sweat. This was something she encountered almost daily at the hospital, with patients who had been wounded in a psychic sense—the emotional breakdowns. As she placed her arm around his shaking shoulders, tears stung Alex's eyes.

"It's okay, okay," she soothed, and wrapped her arms around him. The ability to hold Jim when he needed someone flowed through Alex. She held him with her woman's strength, whispering soft, broken words near his ear as he collapsed against her. His arms went around her, and she felt him holding onto her as if he were a man drowning in an ocean of terror that she couldn't see, but could sense.

Alex's strained voice began to break through Jim's nightmare. One moment he was watching Kim running toward him with the grenade in her hand, smiling. The next, Jim felt the softness of Alex, her arms holding him, until the realization that he was safe impinged upon his splintered senses. Each stroke of her trembling hand against his head and shoulders took a little more of the nightmare away. Each movement made him aware that he was here, with Alex. Jim's arms tightened around her small form, and he took a deep, ragged breath into his lungs.

"That's it, breathe deeply. Just let the nightmare go, Jim. You're safe...safe...."

The flannel of her gown was damp with his tears. He pressed his face into her luxuriant hair, the scent alluring. Alex was here with him. He was alive, not dead. And he was safe. Oh, God, he was safe. And then he tensed. He felt Alex's lips on his sweaty brow, her small, trembling hands framing his face. Her softened moan, her lips touching him and miraculously easing his agony, flooded through him like a river of intense heat and light.

Blindly, Jim straightened and captured Alex in his arms. Kim's death was all he could remember, all he could feel and hear. As he wildly sought and found Alex's mouth, he plundered her, wanting to drown himself in the splendor of her as a woman, as someone so alive and intrinsic to him that he couldn't conceive of living without her. Her mouth was ripe, responsive and eager beneath his exploration. Groaning, lost in the beauty of her, of her need matching and meeting his own, Jim absorbed all of Alex, as if they could magically blend into each other and become one if he kissed her long enough, deeply enough.

His hands trembling as he helped Alex out of the flannel nightgown, Jim ran his fingers across her in awe. Her skin was a velvet field to investigate, to become mesmerized and entangled within. As he ran his fingers down her small shoulder and cupped her breast, he felt her press against him. Her fingers dug frantically into his shoulders, broadcasting her need of him, of his continued quest of her. All the love, all the yearning and longing that he'd stored up for so many months burst free. Leaning down, he captured the rosy peak of her nipple and drew it into his mouth.

A cry jagged through Alex and she tensed along his hard, naked body. The demand increased as he suckled her, and sobs of pleasure tore from her lips. There was such beauty, such reverence in each of his caresses. Alex didn't know how to make love, but she surrendered to her own sense as a woman who needed her man in all ways. As his hand lingered across her rounded belly, the thought of carrying his child had never seemed stronger or more right to her. Any guilt over social demands dissolved within Alex. She understood now, on a primal level, that Jim needed her in this moment. As his hand slid downward to the apex of her thighs, she moaned. Moving his fingers toward the curve of her flesh, he stroked her until the burning fire threatened to consume her, and Alex began to realize just how healing loving could be—not for just Jim, but for herself.

As he eased her down on the bed, on her back, Alex opened her eyes. The tension, the need in Jim's face was undeniable, and she smiled softly as she placed her arms around his shoulders. At that exquisite moment, as he lifted her hips to meet and join with his, Alex thought how silly she had been about her love, worrying about so many extraneous things. Love was the answer, she realized humbly as she leaned upward to capture his mouth.

"I need you," Jim rasped thickly, holding her shimmering gray gaze. "I need you...."

With a quiver, Alex nodded. There was such a flow of love between them, a tangible feeling, that she instinctively raised her hips to meet his thrust. A little cry of surprise, the pressure of him entering her, gave way to relief as he plunged deeply within her. She felt him freeze and hold her as if she were some fragile object ready to break at an instant's notice. Somewhere in her hazy mind of spinning joy and euphoria, Alex realized that Jim was afraid he was going to hurt her.

"Love me," she pleaded, her voice cracking with emotion. "Just love me, Jim."

Jim nodded once, holding his body tensely, under steel control above her. The last thing he ever wanted to do was give Alex more pain. He knew he wasn't the most experienced of lovers. His bumbling attempts might create agony for her. He lay there, his body trembling with need, wanting to be scorched and transformed by her loving form. The softness of her smile and the teasing movement of her hips broke his fear barrier.

Sinking against her, Jim gripped the sheets on either side of her head. "I love you," he rasped. "God, I love you with my life, Alex...."

Gently, she slid her arms across his back, feeling complete as never before. "I know you do," she whispered against his ear, and proceeded to draw the tension from him, to draw him into rhythm with herself.

Each rocking motion tore at him. His grip on the sheets increased, and finally he plunged again and again into her, losing himself in her fiery, welcoming confines. With each rhythmic movement, he felt a little less trepidation, a little less suffering, as his grief melted away in her living, pulsing body. Drowning in the heat of her mouth, her questing lips, her tongue torturing him with new awareness of her as a woman, Jim surrendered much of the horror that had haunted him. He felt as if he were experiencing a miracle of rebirth as he tensed, groaned and then released his life deep within her. The moments melded and blended like lightning striking through every particle of his being, until his mind blanked out, and all that was left was a feeling of oneness with Alex. Somewhere in his overwhelmed senses, he heard her give a little cry, tense and grip him with all her strength.

As he lay on her afterward, their breathing ragged, their bodies blazing with incandescent heat, he opened his eyes slightly. Worried that he might hurt Alex with his weight, Jim eased away from her.

"No..." Alex reached for him. "I like you on me, don't leave," she whispered.

It was easy to cover her, to protect her with his body. "You feel so good to me," he said thickly, kissing her brow, her nose, her cheek and finally, those ripe lips. "I feel so weak."

"Me, too." Alex laughed, luxuriating beneath his weight, his strength against her. She reached up and gently caressed his glistening features. "All the tension in your face is gone," she said with wonder. And his eyes, smoky blue coals banked with desire, no longer held that haunted animal look. Alex was in awe of what their love had done.

"I feel drained," Jim offered as he removed strands of damp dark hair from her brow. "But a good kind of drained, if that makes any sense."

Alex nodded. "Why did we wait so long?"

He smiled and leaned down to kiss her lips. "I don't know. Maybe I was afraid...."

"We both were," Alex said softly. She framed his face. "I didn't know if you loved me or not, Jim."

He shook his head. "I always did."

"But you never said it—until now."

Realizing Alex was right, Jim eased himself off her, then brought her alongside him. Retrieving the covers, he pulled them up and over them. Alex snuggled into his arms, and he felt like a man who had captured heaven and made it his. "I'm sorry," he rasped against her hair. "At first, in Nam, I thought your love was born of the stress we were under, Alex. And after the rescue, when you were in Da Nang, I figured it was out of obligation." He sighed. "I guess I was scared to wish, to hope that you might really love this Missouri country boy."

Alex raised her head and held his dark gaze. She caressed his shoulder. "I love the man I saw from the beginning. It didn't matter what state he was from."

He nodded. "I'm beginning to understand that now, Alex. I was confused, mixed up inside myself. I'd murdered a little girl so I could live. For what? From the moment I did it, I didn't want to live. And then you dropped into my life. I couldn't let you die. You were too courageous, too much a fighter, so it forced me to change my mind again. I knew, taking you back after that bombing raid, that I was going to prison." He smiled a little and leaned over to kiss her lips. "But you were worth it. You showed me a rare kind of courage that I wanted to have. I know you probably didn't realize all that you did for me, Alex."

She shook her head. "No... I had no idea."

"I saw getting you to safety as a way to atone a little bit for taking Kim's life. And I knew that I had to pay for Kim's passing. Looking back on it all, Alex, I wouldn't change one thing that happened. I can never bring Kim back to her family. And I'll spend the rest of my life remembering her, and trying to atone. You helped me get on another track, too. I know with study, with hard work, I can do it. I made a promise to myself that if I survived Long Binh, that if I got the chance, I'd go on to help others who found themselves in their own kind of hell."

"Psychology's a good place for you, then," Alex agreed. "You can help a lot of people by becoming a therapist."

"That's what I want to be, gal. I know I'm not book learned properly, but I've got the time and the desire. Both those things will get me where I want to go. Plus—" Jim smiled down at her "—I have you."

"You've always had me, Jim McKenzie...from the very beginning."

With a sigh, Jim lay down and pressed Alex against him. Just her arm across his chest, her head resting against his shoulder, brought an incredible sense of contentment. "Go to sleep," he told her. "Tomorrow's a new day. It's our beginning."

Chapter Twelve

Alex awoke slowly, sunlight streaming in the windows of the living room and across the bed. Wrapped in the euphoria of loving Jim, she lay savoring the feelings. But as she drew out of the folds of the twilight of sleep, Alex realized that Jim was gone. She sat up, the covers pooled around her hips. He was gone. On the pillow next to her was a handwritten note. Alex reached over, her heart thudding heavily in her breast. The note was from Jim.

Dear Alex,
   I didn't have the heart to wake you up to tell you I was going to be gone for a little bit. I'll be back, gal.

Love, Jim

Relief swept through Alex. Why did she feel insecure? Frowning, she petted Thomasina, who lay nearby on the bed. Still, she couldn't shake the feeling of losing Jim. She got up, struggled into her granny gown and looked at her watch. It was nearly ten o'clock! This morning there was no hurry to get to work—it was the first day of her vacation. Again Alex tried to put aside the uneasy feeling stalking her.

Jim had made coffee and placed an empty cup out beside it for her. His thoughtfulness was a wonderful surprise. Sitting at the table struggling to wake up, still caught in the embrace of loving Jim the night before, Alex tried to tame her mussed hair into a semblance of order. Maybe a hot shower would help her get rid of the fear deep within her. She missed Jim acutely. The thought of waking up in his arms was like a dream come true. Jim loved her no matter how unsettled she felt this morning.

Alex took her shower and chose a pale yellow long-sleeved cotton blouse, a pair of jeans and comfortable low-heeled leather shoes. The glow she felt inwardly from loving Jim continued, and her happiness warred with the fear that refused to leave. Allowing her hair to swing loose and free about her shoulders, Alex put on a bit of perfume, then went to the kitchen to make herself a late breakfast.

Near eleven o'clock, Jim returned. Alex was washing up the dishes in the kitchen when he entered.

"You're up," Jim teased. He smiled as Alex turned around. How could he tell her how beautiful she looked, so clean, with a glow to her eyes and cheeks?

Holding up a bouquet of red roses, he walked over to where she stood smiling.

"These are for you," he whispered, handing her the roses.

Touched, Alex took the bouquet and held it carefully. "Thank you...." She leaned up to kiss his cheek. Alex was surprised and pleased as he framed her face with his hands and leaned down to capture her mouth. His kiss was deep, molten and exploring. She felt herself tremble and moved into his arms, the bouquet caught between them. There was such strength coupled with control as he claimed her. As he tunneled his fingers through her hair, he gently broke the kiss and smiled down into her eyes.

"I love you, Alex Vance. You're a woman any man would be proud to keep company with."

All she could do was drown in the brilliant blue of his eyes, now clear of all haunted looks. Touching his recently shaved cheek, she smiled at him. "And I love you, with all my heart, my soul...."

Looking down at the roses, Jim grinned. "We're going to turn these flowers to mush if we keep this up."

With a startled laugh, Alex took a step away from him. "I think you're right. They're lovely, Jim." She leaned over and inhaled their delicate fragrance. "And they smell so good!"

Pleased that she liked his gift, Jim felt on top of the world. "You're like them, you know? Purty as a spring morning, fresh smelling and reminding me of happier times, better days."

Alex held his dancing gaze, feeling privileged at seeing a side of him she'd never witnessed. "We have so much to catch up on, Jim."

He thrust his hands in his pockets. "I know we do, gal."

"You want to know something silly?" She walked over to the cabinet beneath the sink and pulled out a cut glass vase for the roses.

Jim followed her and leaned against the kitchen counter, just enjoying watching Alex. The kiss he'd given her had made him want her all over again. "Nothing you'd say was silly," he chided.

Alex laughed nervously as she filled the vase with water. "This is, believe me. I woke up this morning, and I was afraid. Can you imagine that?" She took a pair of scissors from another drawer and began to cut each rose stem at an angle before placing it in the vase.

Jim could see something lurking in Alex's gray eyes. "What are you afraid of?"

"That's what doesn't make sense, Jim. It's just a vague feeling. Maybe I'm afraid I'll lose you...."

Jim crossed his arms in the gathering silence. "You aren't gonna lose me," he soothed huskily. "When I woke up this morning with you beside me, I felt like the luckiest man in the world." He glanced over at her. "And then, I got real scared," he admitted. "I lay there thinking of all the ways I could lose *you*, gal— every possible combination that could split us apart." He shook his head. "I thought maybe you'd wake up this morning and ask me to leave because I'd made love to you. Or that you were somehow disappointed with me, or—'' he laughed ''—so many other crazy things.''

Alex fixed the last rose in place and put the vase on the table. Then she walked over to Jim, and his arms opened to welcome her. Leaning her head against his chest, her arms about his waist, she whispered, ''Sounds like we had the same fears.''

With a sigh, Jim nodded and kissed her hair. ''I think,'' he said, ''we're both in shock from finally seeing each other, finally fulfilling something we've always wanted. We've both been through hell, gal, and we're so used to getting kicked down to our knees that what we share this moment seems like an impossible dream come true.''

''I know,'' Alex said, her voice muffled against his shirt, ''I'm afraid it will all end.'' Her voice broke. ''And I don't want it to.''

''Shh, it's all right, sweet woman of mine.'' Jim kissed her hair, her cheek, then placed his fingers beneath her chin. As Alex raised her head and he met her tear-filled gaze, he smiled gently. ''Only an act of God will split us apart, Alex. Believe that. Know it. I do.''

Just then, the doorbell rang. Alex frowned. She quickly wiped the tears from her eyes as Jim released her to answer it. ''Who could that be?'' she muttered.

''I don't know. Expecting any friends?''

''No.'' Alex's heartbeat accelerated with dread. She had no explanation for the apprehension she felt as she crossed the living room to answer the door. Belatedly, she realized she hadn't made up the couch yet, and the bed, with its tangle of blankets and sheets, was in full view.

Jim stood in the living-room doorway, his arms crossed over his chest. The look of worry on Alex's face concerned him. Whatever fear she felt was real.

Alex opened the door. Her jaw dropped. "Father!"

Hiram Vance stood on the doorstep in his dark pin-striped suit, his black overcoat on his arm and an expensive leather briefcase in his left hand. His face was grim.

"Alex."

Alex's heart seemed to shatter at the anger on her father's pugnacious face. "Wh-what are you doing here?"

His jaw set. "Why shouldn't I be here? You're my daughter. I just happened to be in the area and thought I'd drop by. May I come in?"

Starting to tremble, Alex opened the door wide. She didn't have time to say anything to Jim, who came forward to stand at her side, settling a hand on her shoulder.

Her father glared at him. He eyed him for a long moment. "I recognize you from the newspaper articles, McKenzie." Vance flung his glare back to Alex. "What's he doing here, Alex?" he ground out.

Alex shut the door, feeling terribly torn. Her gaze moved to Jim, whose features had hardened—just as they had in the jungle of Vietnam. His eyes narrowed with an intensity that frightened her. Instinctively, Alex stepped between the two men. The indignation and rage in her father's face were unmistakable.

"I—"

"How could you let this cowardly bastard into your house?"

Jim's grip on Alex's trembling shoulder tightened. "Mr. Vance, why don't you let your daughter answer one question before you fire the next salvo?"

Hiram Vance's lips pulled away from his teeth. "Shut up."

"Stop it!" Alex cried. She pulled from Jim's protective grasp and faced her father. "How dare you come in here like this! I haven't done anything wrong, Father. And don't you *dare* call Jim a coward. He—"

"I'm ashamed of you, Alex," Hiram breathed savagely. "You're consorting with a lowlife!"

"I am not!" Alex sobbed.

"Alex," Jim whispered harshly, "stand aside. This is between me and him." Gently, he moved Alex to one side, his heart breaking to see her cry. He rounded on Vance.

"You have no right busting in here and yelling at your daughter, Mr. Vance, when it's me you really want."

"I want *you* out of her life, McKenzie," Hiram snarled. He looked over at the unmade bed. "And it's obvious you plan on hanging around for a while. Let me make this very clear. I don't like you, I don't like your kind, and you're not the right man for my daughter. Not now. Not ever."

Jim controlled himself as never before. The congressman's face was a livid red. He saw the man's fists cocked, ready to strike him. "You don't run my life, Vance. And you don't run Alex's, either. She's old enough to make up her own mind about who she wants in her life.''

Alex felt buffeted by her father's attack. "H-how did you know Jim was here?''

Vance snorted violently. "I've had one of my assistants keeping tabs on him.'' He glared over at McKenzie. "I'd hoped that intercepting those damned letters would do the trick—''

Alex gasped, her eyes becoming round. "You—you stopped my letters from reaching Jim?''

"That's right.''

"That's tampering with mail, Vance. You're supposed to be upholding this country's laws, not breaking them,'' Jim countered.

"Where you're concerned, McKenzie, I'd stop at very little to make sure you stay out of my daughter's life.'' His voice dropped into a sneer. "You're nothing but a dirt-poor Missouri hillbilly—barely a high school graduate. And you refused to fight for your country. I'm not going to allow my daughter to consort with a yellow belly like you—''

"Stop it!'' Alex shrieked. She stabbed blindly at her father's chest with her index finger. "I don't care if he's poor! He's got more decency and better morals than you ever had, Father. And I don't care where he's from or what his damned school grades were! You're wrong about Jim not serving this country! How can you forget that he spent two years in Vietnam with the recons? How can you forget he's got two purple hearts and a silver star for bravery? Damn you,'' she sobbed, backing away from him. "I see the good in Jim. You only want to see the bad!''

Hiram glowered at his daughter. "He's not good enough for a congressman's daughter. You can do better."

"Get out, Father." Alex stood rigidly, her voice oddly low and off-key. "Get out of my house. If you can't talk civilly and be mature about this, I don't want to speak to you anymore. Not until you calm down."

Hiram put his hands on his hips. "You forget, Alex, it was my money that put you through nursing school. I paid for everything."

"You don't own her, Vance," Jim whispered caustically. "And if you think you can hang money over her head to make her come into line with your beliefs, I'll make damn sure every last cent is refunded to you no matter how long it takes."

Hiram gave him a strange look. "What that hell are you talking about?"

Jim moved over and placed his arm around the distraught Alex. He ached for her. "My intentions toward Alex are honorable. I love her, and I intend to ask her to marry me."

Alex took in a ragged breath and glanced up at Jim's grim features. The words she'd wanted to hear but never dared hope for had been spoken. She saw her father's eyes grow huge in disbelief.

"Alex?" Hiram demanded harshly, "is that true? Are you seriously thinking about marrying this—this coward?"

Her heart squeezed with such pain that it took everything Alex had to stand before her indignant father. She felt Jim's arm tighten around her, as if to give her silent support. "Father, I've loved Jim since I met him."

"But look what he's done!" Vance roared.

A strange peace flooded Alex, as if all her fear suddenly dissolved. In its place was a sureness she'd never before experienced. "What's he done?" she quavered. "He's a man who has paid triple the price that anyone should going to war! He served with bravery and honor for two years before experiencing a tragedy beyond most people's worst nightmare. War did it, Father. Jim didn't. Please, can't you understand that he—"

"No, Alex," Jim said thickly, "don't try and defend me. It's no use." He held Hiram's glare. "You think whatever you want of me, Mr. Vance. I love your daughter with my life. But I doubt there's any way I could prove it to your satisfaction."

"I can't believe this, Alex," Vance rattled. "You're actually going to marry him?"

Jim looked down at Alex's taut, washed-out features and saw the terrible suffering in her dark gray eyes.

"Jim and I have a lot of things to catch up on before we cross that bridge, Father. We need time to get to know each other."

"Well," Hiram said as he strode toward the door, "if you marry this coward, Alex, you're as good as disowned. I won't have my daughter marrying a man with a bad conduct discharge! Politically, it would be disastrous. I hope you make the right decision."

The door slammed shut. Alex jumped outwardly and shut her eyes. She felt Jim's arms go around her. Her knees grew weak, and she sank against him.

"I'm sorry, so sorry," Jim whispered.

"No," Alex choked, "I owe you an apology, Jim."

He kissed her damp cheek. "Maybe he's right, Alex. I told you last night that my past will always stay with me. This is the kind of thing you could run into if you stay around me." He caressed her sleek sable hair, sharing her anguish. "I don't want to make you hurt any more than you already have, gal."

Grimly, Alex looked up at him. All she had to do was see the hurt and torture in Jim's eyes to know the answer. "Jim, we've survived the war."

"What about the people who would know about me? Judge my past?"

"They aren't people I want to know," Alex whispered. She caressed his hardened features, knowing how much her father's hurled insults had hurt Jim. "If people can't see your goodness, your honesty, then that's their problem, not ours."

He held her tightly for a long time, unable to speak, only to feel intensely. "You're so small, yet you've got a backbone of steel," he said against her ear.

"No more so than you," Alex said.

"Nothing's been easy for us, has it?"

"No."

He gazed down into her sad eyes. "I didn't mean to bring up marriage. I—well, someday, I planned to ask you to marry me if things worked out between us, Alex."

She nodded. "I'm glad to know."

He rallied beneath her warm look. "Yeah?"

"Yeah," she teased huskily, and then threw her arms around his neck. Alex felt his strength, his love. "Your past," she said, "is past. Jim, you're starting out a whole new life. You've got goals, good ones, and a dream."

Holding Alex tightly, he nodded. "I've dreamed so big, I'm afraid it's never going to come true."

With a shake of her head, her eyes pressed shut as she clung to him, she quavered, "Never let that dream go. We'll make it work. We'll hold on to it together."

Smiling gently, Jim squeezed her tightly, pressing a kiss to her shining hair. "Together," he promised.

Chapter Thirteen

Alex was just getting off work when she saw Jim sauntering toward her from the bank of elevators. As always, her heart started hammering in anticipation. She quickened her pace. Since they'd returned from their trip to Missouri, taken the week he'd come back from Vietnam, the changes in him had been remarkable. Jim had two part-time jobs and was working hard to save enough money to start college in January. He'd already applied for several scholarships and grants and talked to a counselor about his chosen field of psychology.

Jim was dressed casually, as always, in jeans, a long-sleeved plaid shirt and a beat-up leather jacket. His dark hair had grown slightly—although it was still military short, in Alex's opinion. His boyish smile of welcome as she approached sent a sheet of warmth and longing through her. Since her father's visit, they'd grown closer, if that was possible. Alex was amazed at the way adversity had sent them down a path not only of self-discovery, but of discovery of each other. It had been one of the happiest times of her life, and one of the saddest. Her father refused to talk to her about Jim at all, and her mother was caught in the middle. Alex had received letters from her two brothers, but they had been letters more of curiosity than condemnation. Alex had spent a great deal of time writing back to them about Jim. To her disappointment, neither had responded. But perhaps it was because they were deployed far out at sea on their naval carriers.

Jim stopped and placed his hands on his hips. "If you aren't a sight for sore eyes, gal." With a low whistle, he caught Alex's hand and squeezed it warmly.

Alex laughed and smiled. "Hi, stranger. What a nice surprise." Jim's appearance felt like an unexpected gift.

Walking her to the elevators, Jim shrugged. "I guess I had that coming, didn't I?" They saw each other once a week. Usually, on that free evening, Alex cooked for him, because he loved home-cooked meals. They would allow themselves the luxury of curling up together to watch television over a bowl of popcorn, snuggled in each other's arms. Jim would stay the night and leave the next morning for his first job.

"How are the jobs coming along?" Alex asked as she followed him into the empty elevator.

"Boring, but I just keep thinking of the books and tuition they'll pay for. It's a decent trade-off," Jim said. The instant the doors whooshed shut, Jim took Alex into his arms. He saw the greeting in her gray eyes, and the smile that blossomed across her lips as he leaned down to kiss her. There was such warmth and intensity to her as she moved into his waiting arms.

"Mmm," Alex whispered as she drew back a few inches to look at him. "You are something else, Jim McKenzie."

He grinned. "Glad you think so, Miss Vance. I talked to your supervisor earlier today, and she's agreed to give you the next four days off. How about that?"

Alex smoothed out her uniform, her entire body still tingling from his heated welcome kiss. "Oh?"

His eyes twinkling, Jim gave her a pleased look. "Yup. I also talked my two managers into giving me the same time off."

It was December 22, and Christmas was fast approaching. Alex was stymied. "What's going on, Jim?"

Jim pulled two airline tickets from his jacket pocket. "Here. Merry Christmas, gal."

Perplexed, Alex opened one of the tickets as they walked out of the elevator toward the parking lot at the rear of the hospital. "Tickets, Jim?"

"Looks like it. Go on, read them. What do they say?"

Alex stopped at the rear door and read the ticket closely. "Round trip tickets from Portland to Missouri."

Jim grinned. "So would you like to go home over Christmas with me, Miss Alexandra Vance?"

Thrilled, she laughed. "I'd love to!"

"Good." Jim opened the door for her and they walked out arm in arm. The evening was cool, the wind blustery and the skies cloudy.

"I see that glimmer in your eyes, Jim McKenzie. That means trouble."

Jim had taken a bus to the hospital from his restaurant job so he could drive Alex home in her station wagon. Once in the car, he put his arms around her. "I thought it was time," he told her seriously.

Alex sat very still. "Time? For what?"

"Us." Gently he threaded his fingers through her hair, savoring the natural beauty that radiated from her.

Alex understood what Jim meant. Their time together had been severely limited, the moments they were able to share like bright spots of sunlight. "I'd love to go home with you over the holiday," she whispered.

He smiled happily. As they shut the doors and began the drive home, he said, "I've got one more surprise."

Alex glanced over at him. "I don't know if I can take all this good news all at once, Jim." Gripping his hand, she asked, "What is it?"

"I don't know if I told you that, when I was up on that hill with Captain Johnson, Gunny Whitman, the second in command, was badly wounded. When my court-martial went down, the gunny wasn't around to testify on my behalf." Jim grimaced. "If he had been, Lieutenant Breckenridge felt the other charge against me would have been dropped. Captain Johnson's story about my behavior was mostly lies, but I didn't have Whitman to prove it."

Jim held her gaze. "My skipper called me today. He's over here on leave, getting married to a lady he's known for five years. He called to tell me that Gunny Whitman is well enough to give his story to the appeals board." His hand tightened on Alex's fingers. "If the board believes the gunny, then it's possible that my sentence will be overturned. I could get back my rating as corporal, and all my back pay."

Shaken, Alex whispered, "Jim, that's wonderful!"

"There's more," he said, his voice mirroring hope. "Lieutenant Breckenridge said the bad conduct discharge would be lifted. The board will more than likely give me an honorable discharge or a medical one. Either way, it would mean I could get my GI benefits back to help pay my college tuition."

"And you wouldn't have to work two jobs," Alex added excitedly. "How soon will you know?"

"The skipper said the board would convene in early January. I don't have to be present. The board will review all the old testimony, hear Whitman's side, and make a decision. I'll be notified by mail."

"What a great New Year's gift."

"Now, don't count on this, gal," he warned heavily. "What it comes down to is the board believing

Captain Johnson's testimony or believing Gunny Whitman.''

Alex knew that the gunny sergeants in the Marine Corps served as fulcrum points between officers and enlisted men. If there was such a thing as a backbone to the corps, it came in the guise of the gunnys. "They'll believe Whitman," she said fervently. "I just *know* they will."

He grinned. "I hope you're right...."

Jim was in the kitchen helping Alex make dinner when the phone rang. She dried her hands on a towel and picked up the wall phone near the kitchen door.

"Hello?"

"Alex, this is your father."

Her heart plunged. His voice sounded ragged and edgy. Since that fateful day he'd shown up unexpectedly, she'd talked only to her mother. Her mouth suddenly dry, Alex glanced over at Jim, who was still busy chopping lettuce.

"Father. It's nice to hear from you."

Jim looked up sharply, the knife stilled in midair. He saw Alex's face blanch of all color, her eyes go dark. Compressing his lips, he turned and waited to hear the rest of the conversation.

"Alex, your mother and I want you home for the **holiday. I've ordered** one of my assistants to get you a **plane reservation** on TWA for two days from now."

Jim saw the anguish in Alex's eyes. Automatically, he moved to her side and placed a steadying hand on her shoulder. He could see the devastating effect of whatever had been said. What was her bastard of a father up to now? He tried to control his anger and remain still while Alex spoke.

"Father...I can't—"

"Why, Alex? Because of *him?*

"Even if I could come home, he'd be with me, Father."

"We invited you, not him!"

"Please," Alex begged, "don't start shouting at me. It doesn't help anything!"

"I'm sorry, Alex. Look, there are other reasons for you to come home."

"What? Is something wrong with Mother?"

"No. It's Case. He's been given orders to ship over with his marine squadron. Shortly after Christmas, he's leaving for Da Nang. He'll be flying F-4 Phantoms out of there in support activities with the ground forces."

"Oh, dear...."

"You've got to come home, Alex. This will be your last chance to see Case before he ships out. He wants to see you, but not with McKenzie."

Alex felt Jim's hand on her shoulder. "First of all, I've got plans to go home with Jim to visit his folks in Missouri," Alex said hoarsely. "We've already got airline tickets...." Her voice dropped in anguish.

"So cancel the damned tickets, Alex! You belong at home with us. With your older brother! What if Case gets killed in action? You will have missed the opportunity—"

Alex covered her mouth with her hand to hold back a cry. The very real possibility of Case getting killed slammed through her. She struggled and found her voice. "Father, that's not fair! It hurts me. I—I won't come home. Not for Christmas."

"Dammit, Alex, don't be so stubborn! That man isn't your shadow!"

"No," she rasped unsteadily, "he isn't." Alex was well aware of Jim's dark, concerned look for her. "But I happen to love him, Father, and he's part of my life whether you approve or not."

"Well, Case is going to be terribly disappointed in you, Alex. You're forsaking your own brother for that bastard! What kind of daughter are you, anyway?"

Pain ripped through Alex. Gathering every bit of her shredded courage, she whispered, "I love Case very much, Father. If he wants to see me before he goes, he can come to Missouri. Or he can call. Mother has Mrs. McKenzie's phone number."

"I'm very disappointed in you, Alex."

"I know. I've known it all my life."

The phone line went dead. Her father had hung up on her.

Alex shut her eyes.

Jim took the receiver from her hand and placed it back on the wall. Gently, he gripped her by the shoulders. "What happened?"

Blinking back her tears, Alex tried to smile, but couldn't. She told Jim everything, watching as hurt came into his eyes. Knotting her fists against his chest, she cried, "This isn't fair, Jim! It just isn't fair! Why can't Father accept you, and how I want to live my life?"

"Because," Jim said grimly, gathering Alex in his arms, "he wants to control you like he does the rest of his family." After holding her for a long time in silence, he looked down at her. "Would you rather go home to see Case? I wouldn't mind."

Her love for him tripled. "I don't know what to do, Jim. Father's pride is in the way, but so is mine. I refuse to go home without you. And yet, do I refuse to see Case, to not say goodbye to him?" Alex buried her face in the folds of his shirt, hearing his heart—a steady, calming beat—against her ear.

"Sweet woman, whatever your decision, I'll stand by you. Seeing Case is more important. He doesn't deserve to be penalized just because of your father—or because of my actions."

"Don't say that!" Alex looked up through her veil of tears. "This isn't your fault. I don't accept that, Jim. I never will. Remember? I'm the one who was out there in that jungle with you. I'm not about to abandon you in face of my damned father's emotional blackmail. And what I hate most is that Case is a pawn in all of this—that Father is using him."

"He's using Case to hurt you because you love me, Alex."

Miserably, Alex wiped her eyes. "I know it," she said, her voice wobbling.

It was on the tip of his tongue to say that Hiram Vance loved no one but himself, that he manipulated the members of his family like a puppeteer, and the family merely reacted in a knee-jerk fashion. Anger, hot and startling, sizzled through Jim. Alex was a victim of her father's hatred of him. As much as Jim wished that his past wouldn't interfere, it was, once again.

"You can go home, Alex."

She shook her head. "No! I won't give Father the satisfaction. I won't!" Gazing up at him, Alex whispered, "I want to go home with you. We deserve this time together. I love your mother and father almost as if they were my own."

"Okay," Jim said, his voice cracking, "we'll go home—together."

"Welcome, welcome, welcome!" Tansy McKenzie called from the wooden porch of their Ozark cabin, surrounded by trees that had shed their leaves for the coming winter. Dressed in a simple cotton dress and bright red apron, the petite woman had never looked happier.

Alex climbed out of the rented car and waved. Some of her depression lifted as Jim's mother, who was in her mid-sixties, moved gingerly off the porch. The evening was upon them, the sky a darkening blue and cloudless, the air brisk.

"Hi, Ma!" Alex greeted her excitedly as she shut the car door. As she walked toward Tansy, Alex wished with all her heart that she could experience such obvious love and warmth from her own family. But somehow, as she reached out and hugged Jim's mother, Alex felt the invisible load she carried on her shoulders lighten.

"Oh, you look wonderful!" Tansy bubbled, holding Alex at arm's length. "Lordy, you're more purty than ever before!" she declared, her eyes twinkling. She released Alex as Jim approached. "Hello, son. Welcome home!"

Jim embraced his mother. He was so tall and lean in comparison to Tansy.

Alex smiled her welcome as John McKenzie approached. As always, he was dressed in bib overalls and a plaid flannel shirt. His head was bald, and he wore an ancient pair of spectacles far down on his hawklike nose. It was the merriment in his eyes that made Alex smile even wider.

"Hi, Mr. McKenzie. Merry Christmas." Alex offered her hand. A handshake was all she had ever shared with Jim's reserved father. Unlike Tansy, John remained somewhat distant. Alex respected his need for formality, so it was with great surprise—and pleasure—that she saw the tall, lanky man open his arms.

"Welcome home, Alexandra," he said gruffly, hugging, then quickly releasing her.

Welcome home. The words rang sweetly, and Alex beamed. "Thank you, Mr. McKenzie."

"Call me John. No sense standin' on ceremony."

"I'd love to," Alex admitted, surprised yet thrilled by his decision. She saw John's severe-looking features soften even more as Jim approached. Alex held back tears as she saw the warmth, pride and love pass between father and son. When John McKenzie embraced his son, it was with enthusiasm and obvious delight. If Alex had any doubts about her decision to come to the Missouri Ozarks for Christmas, they were laid to rest now. As she looked around, she realized there wasn't a dry eye among them.

Sniffing, Tansy gripped Alex's hand. "Well, ya'll come in! It's chilly out here, and we've got a roarin' fire inside. Come!"

The interior of the cabin was filled with wonderful odors, and Alex smiled over at Jim as they took off their coats.

"I'm starved, Ma."

Tansy poked at her son's ribs. "Jim, yore lookin' a mite thin. Four days of home cookin' is what you need."

"Son, you look like a starvin' cow brute to me," John noted wryly as he ambled toward the living room.

Jim put his arm around Alex and grinned. "Well, if it weren't for this gal, I'd look a lot worse, believe me."

Tansy nodded and winked over at Alex. "Honey, will you help me set the table? The pheasants are done cookin', and I've got everything timed for half an hour from now."

"Pheasants?"

"Shore," John said, settling back in a black-walnut rocker near the potbellied stove. "I went huntin' wild turkey this mornin', but they outsmarted me. A couple of dumb pheasants sittin' in my neighbor's cornfield didn't, though."

"I've never had pheasant," Alex admitted, content with country living.

"Tastes better than any ol' store-bought chicken, that's for sure," Tansy said as she led her to the kitchen. She opened a drawer and handed Alex a green apron. "Here, put this on a'fore you get food all over that purty outfit of yores."

Alex blushed. Her jeans and soft pink sweater were hardly special. She looked across the small kitchen, the counter space filled with delicacies. "I'm so glad to be here, Ma."

Blotting her eyes with a handkerchief, Tansy smiled. "You belong here, Alexandra."

Alex smiled, feeling teary-eyed herself as she took the flatware handed to her. The table was in the kitchen, hand hewn from walnut and carefully crafted. The cloth, a pale yellow linen, was obviously old and lovingly cared for. Putting the heavy ceramic plates at each place, Alex fell into a kind of unspoken rhythm with Tansy.

"Me and Pa were hopin' like the dickens you two young 'uns could make it back here for the holiday," Tansy said with a smile.

Alex watched as Jim's mother brought three lightly browned pheasants out of the oven. The kitchen was hot from the wood-burning iron stove. Freshly baked bread sat up above in the warmer.

"I agree with Jim," Alex said, helping move the stuffed birds to a huge white platter. "There's no place like home for the holidays."

"Yes, and with the way that boy of ours has been workin', I've been worried. He's not putting on much weight."

No one worked harder than Jim. Alex patted Tansy's tiny shoulder. "He's driven."

"I know, I know. It's as if his past is a shadow on his heels or somethin'." Tansy stood back and looked at the birds, a pleased expression on her thin features.

"Those two jobs he has get him up at six o'clock, and he doesn't get home until midnight," Alex confided. She brightened and met Tansy's worried blue eyes. "Did you know Jim just got a scholarship?"

"No!"

Alex laughed. "I think he'll be able to quit his night job soon because of the grant money."

"Maybe things are starting to turn around for you two young 'uns." Then Tansy muttered, "I still worry. Here, would you like to carry in the birds? John sure peppered the heck out of them. You'd think he was afraid they might fly away after the first burst of buckshot. No, he had to pepper them twice. I hope I got all those pellets dug out of them 'fore I baked them. Just tell everyone to eat carefully. I don't want no broken tooth complaints."

Before long, the table was ladened with food, and they all sat down. Tansy said a short prayer and everyone settled down to eat. She'd prepared mouthwatering homemade bread, black walnut stuffing, gooseberry Jell-O, baked potatoes from the garden out back of the cabin and spiced crab apples with cranberries. Alex didn't realize how hungry she'd become. To her consternation, she ate nearly as much as Jim.

For dessert, Tansy proudly produced a squash pie and freshly whipped cream. Cream, she informed Alex, that had been skimmed off the top of milk produced by Bessy, their guernsey cow. As Alex sat enjoying the food and company, she was struck by the simplicity of the McKenzies as opposed to her own family. Everything on the Vance table would have been catered. The food here tasted better, more alive, and the kitchen was a place of so many mouth-watering fragrances.

Afterward, Tansy herded Alex and Jim out of the kitchen. John lit his corncob pipe, sat down in his rocker near the stove in the living room and listened to the antique radio in the corner by the small, brightly lit Christmas tree. Even now, the McKenzies had no television. Alex tried to help Tansy in the kitchen, but she wouldn't hear of it.

"You go be with Jim, honey. From his letters, you ain't spent much time together 'cause he has to work so hard. You be with him for a while."

Touched, Alex nodded and thanked Tansy. Jim had come from his parents' bedroom opposite the living room, and he had their coats under his arm.

"How about a walk to work off some of that food?" he teased, holding her coat open so that she could slip into it.

Alex laughed. "I feel like one of those stuffed pheasants! A walk's exactly what I need."

Outside, the crisp freshness of the winter air was tinged with the sweetish smell of decaying leaves and other heady scents of late autumn. It had yet to snow. Jim smiled and tucked Alex beneath his arm as they strolled off the creaky wooden porch and onto the dew-laden grass.

Alex inhaled deeply as they moved away from the cabin. There, just above the woods that surrounded the small meadow, a butter-colored full moon loomed huge on the horizon. They stood in each other's arms in silence at its beauty, at the moonlight skimming the tops of the maple, elm, walnut and ash trees.

"It's so beautiful," Alex breathed, glancing up into Jim's shadowed features. Since they'd arrived, his face had lost its tension, and for that, Alex was grateful.

"Full moons are all of that," he whispered, gazing down at Alex. "But what I'm looking at now is even purtier."

Alex stretched up to gently kiss his cheek, then they continued their walk down a well-trodden cow path that led into the fenced meadow. "You make me feel pretty," Alex admitted. "You always have."

"Just being honest," Jim countered seriously. The day was almost gone, a pale strip of blue showing along the western horizon, with a curtain of ebony following on its heels. The air grew even more chilly and their walk was brisk.

"Where are we going?"

"Oh, a special place."

"Tell me about it."

"Raven Holler is what we call it," Jim told her. "It's how the community got its name." They left the meadow and moved into the woods, stepping on the damp, fragrant leaves. "When I was a kid, I used to come here a lot and just daydream. I used to try to imagine what my life was going to be like." He laughed. "Of course, it didn't turn out anything like what I expected."

Alex rested her head on Jim's shoulder. She tightened her arm around his waist. Although they were in bulky winter coats, she craved his closeness. "Is your life better or worse than you imagined?"

Jim steered her down a slight slope. "Much better," he assured her. Easing away, he gripped Alex's hand and helped her negotiate a sudden, steep decline.

Alex could see a small pond of water surrounded by dried grass and a rolling expanse of open land. She sensed something different about Raven Holler as Jim led her over to the pond. Beside the water were two huge limestone rocks.

Jim halted by the water. "Do you feel it?"

She nodded. "What is it?"

He shrugged. "A long time ago, the Cherokee people used to live here. The McKenzies settled here sometime in the mid 1700's, and discovered this place." Jim pointed up to a tall old maple tree, now dead, that hung at an angle over the quiet pond. "The story goes that the raven clan of the Cherokee people lived here until they were killed by the white man's disease, smallpox. This place was sacred to them, and they came here for ceremonies. I can remember as a boy hearing the calls of a raven family and coming here. Those huge black birds used to live up in that tree, bear their young and teach them to fly off it. The hill folk believed Raven Holler was magical."

Jim smiled wistfully. "The story goes that if you have a wish you want to come true, you come here. You lay food at the base of that old maple tree, make your wish and leave. When you come back the next day, if the food gift is gone, then you were granted your wish by the spirits who live here. If the food is still there, well, you didn't get your wish."

Alex sighed. "I love everything about you, about the people here in the Ozarks, Jim. Maybe that's where you got your wonderful romantic streak, your way of looking at life."

"My way of looking at things has caused me a lot of trouble, too," he reminded her wryly.

"Not in my book," Alex said. She turned in his arms and smiled up at him. "So, are we going to make a wish?"

Jim caressed her warm, velvet cheek. "I brought some food. But there's another story, the real reason I brought you here." He held her soft gray gaze. "Because of the magic of this place—a place where wishes come true—every man who wants his gal to say yes to his marriage proposal, comes here. It's been said that when a woman says yes here, the blanket is never split between them."

Touched, Alex whispered, "Blanket split?"

"Sorry." Jim laughed nervously. "That's hill slang for divorce."

Alex gazed at the quiet pool, now beginning to reflect the silver light of the rising full moon. Jim dug into the pocket of his coat and produced a small black-velvet box. Alex's breath snagged. Her heart started to beat hard in her breast.

Jim released Alex, and his long fingers fumbled with the box. Finally, the tiny latch was released. He glanced over at Alex, his own heart pounding.

"I've been saving for this," he told her, his voice unsteady, "and I've been waiting for the right time."

Jim lifted his head and looked around the quiet area. His gaze settled back on Alex's upturned face. "I hope I haven't blown it with you, gal. The way we met, we didn't have time to really know each other, until recently. I felt like it was the right time to ask...." He swallowed hard, the words coming out hoarse. "Will you marry me, Alex? Will you be my wife? My best friend?"

"Oh, Jim..." Alex stared down at the box as he opened the lid. Inside lay an engagement ring set with a small diamond solitaire, and a gold wedding band.

"I know it's not much, Alex. You deserve a much larger diamond—"

"It's perfect," Alex breathed, her voice wobbling as she lightly touched the set. "And so beautiful..." No one knew better than Alex how strapped Jim was for money. His two part-time jobs barely paid for his food, rent and tuition. "How...I mean, this must have cost you so much. How did I afford it at all, Jim?"

"I took a third job."

Alex gave him a distraught look. "Oh, no!"

"Now, don't go getting upset on me, gal. It's only for a little while." Proudly, Jim held the box toward her. "You really like them? I had a hard time trying to decide."

"Like? I love them!" She held the small box in her hand.

"Then...you'll marry me, Alex?"

Tears slipped down her cheeks. "Of course I will, Jim."

Relief deluged Jim, and he took a step back, caught himself, then threw his arms around her. He heard Alex laugh, then sob. Holding her as if he'd never let her go, he rasped, "The magic's still here in Raven Holler."

Kissing him tenderly, Alex finally broke away enough to hold his warm blue gaze. "No, you're the magic, Jim. It's you. Your upbringing."

He frowned and lightly touched Alex's hair. "I'm worried, Alex."

"Why?"

"Well, your family and all..."

"You're marrying me, not my family."

"Still, it's bad blood between me and them, gal. What might the situation do to you over the years? I've tried to understand what it might feel like if my folks hadn't forgiven me and taken me back into their fold." Frustration colored his tone. "Are you sure you want to marry me, Alex?"

With a little laugh, Alex held up the engagement ring. Moonlight glinted off it, like fire blazing through the facets. "Jim McKenzie, are you trying to talk me *out* of marrying you?"

"No," he whispered as he slipped it on her finger, "I'm not. I just want you to be very clear about what's ahead for us."

"Jim, we belong together because of our courage to face our greatest fears. That's what I love most about us—we both realize that making fear our friend instead of allowing it to stop us from growing, is our strongest asset." Gravely, Alex searched his sober features. "If I allowed my fear of my father disowning me to stop me, then I wouldn't be worthy of you, darling. I'll do my best to try and get my family to realize I still love them, even if Father continues to be angry with me."

Understanding, Jim nodded and eased Alex into his arms. "I love you, Alexandra Vance."

"Soon to be Alexandra McKenzie. I love the name. I love the man."

Whispering her name, Jim sought and found her waiting lips, meeting and melding with her on all levels. Their breathing became ragged, their kiss deeper and more hungry. Finally, as they separated, Jim saw the flushed pleasure in Alex's face. He grinned, feeling the horrible weight he'd been carrying for so long slough off his shoulders.

"Want to make a wish now?" he asked, pulling out a small sack of leftovers from the dinner table.

Alex nodded. She followed wordlessly as Jim held her hand and led her around the pool. At the foot of the dead maple tree, he gave her the sack of food.

"Can I tell you what I wish for?" Alex asked breathlessly, her body glowing and warm from his kiss.

He shrugged and put his hands in his pockets. "Sure."

Reverently, Alex placed the food on a huge, twisted root that had been exposed by years of weathering. As she knelt next to it, her hand over the sack, she said, "I wish for peace between our two families."

No one wanted that more for Alex than he did. Jim gathered her into his arms and kissed her for a long, long time. Unwillingly, he finally eased back from her ripe, loving lips and rested his brow against hers. Their breath mingled and became a ragged cloud of vapor in the freezing air.

"That's a good wish," Jim murmured huskily.

Alex closed her eyes. "If only it would come true...."

"I know," he whispered painfully, and slowly turned Alex toward the path that would eventually lead them to the cabin.

Halfway back, Alex smiled. "This is going to be hell, Jim."

"What is?"

She laughed. "Well, we certainly can't sleep together while we're here."

Out of deference to his parents, they had decided not to. Jim grinned and nodded. "You're right."

Alex saw a sparkle in his eyes, a spark of life that had remained there through the darkest of times. "You've got that devilish look in your eyes," she teased.

His laughter rolled along the meadow, deep and joyful. Jim grabbed Alex and swung her around and around until she shrieked and their laughter mingled. They clung to each other, so dizzy that they almost fell onto the dewy grass.

"That doesn't mean," he gasped, "that you're not fair game if we go for a nice long walk out in the woods together in the coming days, Miss Alexandra."

She joined in his laughter, the last of the weight and worries she carried dissolving beneath the moon's silvery luminescence. "You're impossible," she giggled, hugging him, her face buried next to his neck.

"Impossible but very much in love with you," he agreed raggedly.

Chapter Fourteen

As Alex and Jim approached the cabin, they saw another car parked in the gravel driveway. Happy as never before, and bursting to show Tansy and John her lovely engagement ring, Alex thought it might be a neighbor who had come calling late.

"I wonder who's here?" she murmured as she climbed the porch steps arm in arm with Jim.

"Don't know. Probably one of Pa's friends coming over to have a bite of Ma's pie." He grinned. "She's famous for her squash pies, you know."

Alex couldn't agree more. She entered through the door that Jim had opened for her. Her smile slipped.

"Case!"

Captain Case Vance stood in the center of the living room, and slowly turned toward them. "Alex?"

Stunned, Alex stood uncertainly just inside the door. Her older brother, who had the same hair and eyes as she did, was dressed in dark brown slacks, a white collegiate shirt and a leather coat with his squadron patch on the front of it, proclaiming him a Marine Corps pilot. His square face and high cheekbones were topped by military-short hair. The laugh lines around his eyes and mouth hinted at his sense of humor. Anxiously, Alex searched his drawn features for some hint of the reason for his unexpected appearance.

Jim shut the door and stood tensely at Alex's side. His parents bracketed Vance with uneasy looks on their faces.

"What's the meaning of this?" Alex asked softly.

Case stood with his hands on his hips, his eyes cool and assessing. His sharpened gaze moved to his sister.

"I came to see you, Alex." And then he nodded in Jim's direction. "And you, too."

Swallowing against her constricted throat, Alex numbly got out of her coat. Her brother was tall, broad shouldered and, in her eyes, terribly handsome. At twenty-eight, he was a captain and proud of flying one of the hottest and most deadly jets in the world, the F-4 Phantom.

"Did Father send you?" she demanded in a strangled tone.

Case shook his head. "No." And then a strained smile pulled at his thinned mouth. "I got here about ten minutes ago and the McKenzies were kind enough to offer me a late dinner."

"You drove here?" Alex couldn't keep the surprise out of her voice. She still wasn't sure why Case was here. He was known to have her father's temper and same obstinate nature. Her stomach was tightly knotted with fear that their private war might touch Jim's vulnerable and innocent family. She moved toward Case, who towered over her.

"I took off this morning from D.C., Alex." Case lifted his head and pinned Jim with a long look. "Just to set the record straight, I'm here on my own. Father was ranting and raving so damned much that I wasn't about to stay under the same roof with him, Christmas or not."

"Why did you come?" Alex held her brother's narrowed gray gaze.

"I'm shipping out two days from now, and Father said you were going to be here, in the Ozarks. I wanted to say goodbye before I left." His hands slipped off his hips and touched Alex's shoulder. "I'm not at war with either of you."

Alex pressed her fingers against her pounding heart and hung her head, the relief she felt making her shaky and momentarily speechless. She sensed rather than saw Jim approach. When she looked up, Jim was offering his hand to her brother.

"I'm Jim McKenzie." Jim fearlessly held Case Vance's gaze, his hand extended in friendship. Would Case be angry? Refuse to shake his hand? He didn't know, but he had to make the offer for Alex's sake, if not for his own.

With a slight, nervous grin, Case thrust his hand forward and gripped Jim's. "So you're the ghost on the Vance radar screen."

"I'm too alive to be much of a ghost, don't you think?" Jim asked wryly. He wanted to like Alex's brother. Confidence radiated from the pilot. He saw a genuine smile tip Case's mouth and they released their handshake grip.

"I think," Tansy interrupted, clearing her throat, "that you young 'uns can sit and talk out in the kitchen. I just put on a fresh pot of coffee." She smiled up at Case. "And I think you could use that dinner we promised you, Mr. Vance."

"Call me Case, ma'am."

Tansy glowed. "Case is a right proper name for you."

The pilot flushed. He glanced over at Alex. "Well, how about it? I think Mrs. McKenzie has a good idea. Shall we convene this UN delegation in the kitchen and clear the air?"

Hope threaded through Alex and she deferred to Jim, whose hand rested protectively on her shoulder.

"Ma was always wise about these things," Jim agreed. "Let's get somethin' in your stomach, and then we'll talk."

Once Tansy had left and Case had eaten his dinner with obvious relish, Alex waited impatiently to talk further. As always, her brother had the ability to put people at ease, telling stories about Marine Corps life. Her intuition told her Case was here for many reasons. She and Jim sat next to each other, hot cups of coffee in their hands. Alex moved her cup nervously.

Case wiped his mouth with the paper napkin and put his plate aside. He poured a hefty amount of sugar and cream into his coffee and stirred it with a spoon.

"You know Father's like a wounded lion around the house," Case began seriously. He glanced at Jim. "In case you didn't know, my father is into heavy drama when things don't go his way."

Jim nodded. "I wouldn't care, but Alex is involved."

"That she is," Case agreed.

"I think we should make something clear to you," Jim said. "Alex and I love each other, and we're going to get married. I don't know why you're here, or in what capacity, Vance, but if this conversation is going to turn ugly, then you and I will discuss things outside—out of Alex's and my folks' earshot. Is that understood?"

Case sat back and raised his black eyebrows. He looked over at Alex and grinned broadly.

"No wonder Father's so upset. He's finally run into somebody he can't control."

She smiled a little. "Despite what you've heard about Jim, he's never been a coward, Case."

"I can tell...." He sighed and planted both his elbows on the table. "All right, McKenzie, here it is straight off my hip. I love my sister very much, although the last couple of years we haven't had the closeness we had before. Father has been dumping a lot of garbage about you on our family, and I got sick and tired of hearing scuttlebutt. He's making Alex out to be some kind of scapegoat, and I won't have it. My sister has always had a good head on her shoulders, and I respect her for the choices she's made in her life. I'm here to see for myself, and make my own judgment about you. If Alex loves you, I've got to think there's something more to you than what Father's letting on. I'm not here to call you names or add insult to injury. I'm just trying to find out what the hell the truth is.''

Alex gripped her brother's large, square hand. "I love you so much, Case. Thanks for saying those things. I—I thought the whole family felt the way Father does about me...us.''

Case muttered a curse under his breath. "Look, if you two have the time, why don't you tell me everything from the beginning. I heard Father's version, as well as the press stories. I just read an article in *Newsweek* that said a gunny sergeant was going to be a witness to Jim's appeal hearing. You have to understand, Alex, that after you crashed and were officially listed as MIA in the Vietnam jungle, all we knew was what the newspapers and television said about your disappearance. After your rescue, the same thing happened. We got only bits and scraps of information. If Buck and I hadn't been stationed on carriers in the Med, we'd have come and sat on your doorstep to find out what the hell was going down, but we couldn't.'' He cradled her hand between his. Giving Jim a sidelong glance, he smiled at Alex. "So, tell me the story.''

"I'll tell you mine, but Jim will have to speak for himself. It's his story, Case, that's most important for you to hear.'' Alex prayed that her brother would understand Jim's decisions and choices.

"Fair enough," Case murmured.

The clock had struck midnight by the time Jim got done with his part of the story. He didn't know who was more drained by the telling of it—he, Alex or, surprisingly, Case. The Marine Corps officer sat there, his skin pale, his eyes bleak, as Jim finished.

With a shake of his head, Case stood up and ran his fingers through his short hair. "Damnation," he whispered, anguish in his voice.

Alex felt strongly for her brother. Despite his arrogance and brashness, Case had a big streak of sensitivity that he hid from the world—most of the time. Tonight, Jim's story had reached inside her brother and shaken him to his core.

Case paced the kitchen, the silence building. "I didn't know," he began lamely. He stopped and faced Jim squarely. "None of the papers or magazines printed any of this information. I didn't know about Kim . . . or your reasons."

"Of course they didn't," Alex said bitterly. "The truth in Jim's case would have been boring as far as the media was concerned. It was more dramatic, and would sell more papers, if Jim were made out to be a villain."

Case shook his head and approached Jim, his features somber. "I'm sorry, McKenzie. I really am. The real story hasn't gotten out to the American people."

Jim shrugged tiredly. He felt utterly drained and in need of Alex. Did she realize what a pillar of strength she was to him? "It's all right, Captain."

"Call me by my first name," Case muttered, coming back over to sit down. He nailed his sister with a dark look. "This is a crime, Alex. The damned press hung Jim. And so did our father. It's a wonder the review process hasn't thrown the whole mess in the can."

"I don't care about the press or the Marine Corps. What I do care about is how Father's behaving."

"I can't believe he doesn't know the truth about Jim's situation. Politicians in his circle of importance have inside info available to them, even when the public doesn't. He had to know."

"Sure he knows," Jim said quietly. "Alex told him the truth when he visited her after her rescue. She told him to his face."

"Then what's his problem?" Case demanded in disbelief. "My God, any person with a conscience would understand your motives. Hell, I do." Then Case had the good grace to blush. "Alex will tell you I'm pretty insensitive and hardheaded most of the time."

Alex gripped her brother's hand. "Not underneath, you're not," she whispered.

"Part of your father's reason for shunning me, or avoiding the truth," Jim offered as he looked around the rustic kitchen, "is because I'm a hillbilly from the Ozarks. I don't think your father wants Alex to marry below her station."

Case snorted violently, his eyes flashing anger. "Love has no prejudice."

"Father has always been concerned with his power, his importance—and maintaining that image. You know that, Case," Alex reminded him softly. "Tell me, does Mother believe him?"

"Mother has been staying out from under. She keeps her opinion, whatever it is, to herself. You know how Father reacts when he doesn't get his way."

"And what about your brother?" Jim asked Case.

"Buck was just as confused as I was. Now that I know the truth, don't think I won't be writing him a nice long letter explaining things."

"When we get back to Portland, we're going to call Mother and Father and tell them we're getting married," Alex warned her brother.

With a sigh, Case nodded. Then he smiled tiredly. "That's going to set Father off again. But that's his problem, Alex. One of these days, he'll get down off his high horse and accept reality. Congratulations are in order."

Alex saw that he meant it. "Thank you...."

"It's late," Jim said, standing up. "Case, why don't you take the couch. Alex, you take my bed up in the attic, and I'll roll up in a sleeping bag next to the stove. We all need shut-eye."

None of them disagreed. When they walked into the living room, all the lights except one had been turned off, and Alex realized Jim's folks were already in bed. As Jim got the blankets and pillows from a hall closet, Alex stood next to her brother near the warmth of the stove. She hugged Case for a long time.

"I like him," Case told her in a low voice as they eased apart. He grinned broadly. "Not that you need my blessing or anything. All three of us kids inherited Father's stubborn nature."

She nodded. "It means a lot to me to know you don't hold Jim's past against him ... us."

Opening his hands, Case murmured, "How can I? His decision is something I would never want to be faced with, Alex. My God, he must live in constant pain with that memory."

"He does," she whispered. She watched as Jim brought out two pillows and several blankets. When he went back to the closet, she said, "I always know when he's seeing it all over again. His eyes go dark, as if he's back in Vietnam. It's a faraway look, a haunted look. When he stays over with me, he sometimes wakes up screaming about Kim.... It's terrible, Case. In some ways, it's eating Jim alive. I try my best to be there for him, to help him." Alex chewed on her lip. "But I don't think love or understanding is enough."

Case squeezed her gently. "With time, some of the horror in Jim will go away," he promised. "Until then, just keep loving him with everything you have, Alex. Your love, more than anything, will get him through this hell."

Exhausted, Alex nodded. "Just be careful in Vietnam, Case. I'd die if you got hurt or shot down...."

"I hope," Case muttered, "I don't ever get shot down and captured by those Commie bastards. That's the thing I fear most." With a shrug of his broad shoulders, Case added, "I don't know what I'd have done if I were in Jim's shoes, Alex."

"If it's any help, I learned that war does only one thing—it makes you aware of your need to survive."

"Well," Case said grimly, "I've got to fly one hundred missions before I can come home. I know I'll find out all about survival."

Worry thrummed through Alex. She looked up at her big brother's shadowed and sober features. A fierce love for him swept through her. "I just want you home safe," she whispered.

Jim glanced over at them as he placed a sleeping bag near the stove. "Let's hit the sack, people. We're all so tired we're ready to keel over. Alex, you want the bathroom first?"

She smiled. "No, you two do your thing. Women are always slower."

"I'll go first," Case volunteered, and he picked up the small leather satchel that sat near the couch.

Alex moved into Jim's arms. With a sigh, she rested against his strong, lanky form. "I love you," she said as she slid her hand across his chest.

"I know you do, gal." Jim pressed a kiss to her cheek. "You were awfully brave tonight. You know that?"

Alex looked up and melted beneath his molten blue gaze. "Me? *You* were!"

"He was your brother, Alex. That's just another thing I love about you—you don't jump to conclusions or get defensive. You let the other person say his piece."

"I'm so glad Case doesn't hate you," Alex said in a wobbly voice.

"With time, maybe," Jim told her, holding her gently in his arms, "the rest of your family will come around the way he has. I'm sure your father will refuse to come to the wedding, gal. I hope you're prepared for that.''

Alex held him tightly, hearing his solid heartbeat beneath her ear. ''I don't want them around if they aren't going to be happy for us, Jim.''

''Time heals all things,'' he soothed, hurting for her. ''If Case came to you, so will Buck, and then your mother. Eventually, your father will, too.''

''I hope so.''

He smiled and gazed down at her soft, flushed features. ''I'm going to miss not having you in my arms tonight, but pretty soon, we're going to change that.''

Alex absorbed his smile, his sincerity. ''What about an April wedding? Here, at your folks' place?''

He lifted his chin and thought about it. ''I know Ma and Pa would love it.''

''What about you?''

''April's a good month, lots of flowers, everything budding out. A new beginning. How about tying the knot down at Raven Holler?''

A sweet joy swept through Alex. She leaned up and kissed him tenderly. ''That's a wonderful idea! The spot is so pretty, Jim. I love it.''

''See?'' he teased. ''The magic of Raven Holler's already working. You put that gift of food at the bottom of the old maple tree and look what happened— your brother showed up to make his peace with us.''

Laughing, feeling lighter and more hopeful than she had in a long time, Alex embraced Jim with a fierceness that paralleled her love for him. ''My love for you is forever,'' she said, her voice filled with tears. ''Forever.''

Epilogue

February 14, 1966

Humming softly, Alex looked at herself in the full-length bedroom mirror. It was Valentine's Day, a special day for her and Jim. Her pale pink silk dress fit her perfectly with its long sleeves, scoop neck and Empire waist. More than anything, Alex loved the long, flowing lines of the knee-length fabric. The pearls around her throat emphasized her flushed cheeks, and she applied a bit of pink lipstick. Jim was going to take her to dinner, and they had so much to celebrate.

The doorbell rang. Thomasina, the cat, leaped up and raced down the hall. Alex smiled, picked up her black leather purse and hurried out of the bedroom.

Although it was cloudy and cool, Jim wore his only suit, a dark blue one, without a raincoat. Alex smiled as she stepped aside to let him into the foyer. In his hand was a bouquet of red roses.

"For you," he said, and leaned down to capture her warm, welcoming mouth.

The scent of the roses combined with Jim's natural scent to make Alex heady with need. She leaned upward, pressing her hands to his chest. As he eased back from her lips, she saw his blue eyes dancing with happiness.

"I love you," Alex whispered.

Jim smiled and handed her the flowers. "You're my life, gal. Here, these roses can't even begin to compare with how purty you are, but they're the closest thing I could find to show you how you look to my eyes."

Taking the roses into the kitchen, Alex smiled gently. "If women only knew how romantic you Missouri men were, I'm sure there would be a run on the state, to capture each and every one of you."

Jim leaned against the counter as he watched Alex arrange the bouquet in a cut glass vase. He smiled. "I'm already hog-tied and spoken for." Her hair was coiffed in a French twist, the soft bangs touching her brows. The dress made him ache for Alex. Lately, since college had started, they'd had no time together—at all.

"You heard anything from Case yet?" Her brother had shipped over to Nam in late December.

Alex took the vase into the living room and set it on the coffee table. "Yes. Finally! He's at Da Nang." She laughed. "And he's having a good time, I guess."

"Oh?"

"He met this nun, a Sister Theo from a local Catholic orphanage. From the sounds of his letter, he'd fall head over heels in love with her this instant if she weren't a nun." Alex laughed. "It serves Case right—he was always chasing the girls and using his fighter-pilot image to coax them into relationships."

Jim smiled and retrieved Alex's coat from the closet. He slipped it across her shoulders. "Payback can be a son of a gun."

Chuckling, Alex nodded. "Case spends his free time, what little there is, with the kids of the orphanage. He *loves* kids! And I guess they love him, too. But I kinda think he hangs around that orphanage mostly because of Sister Theo. From his description, she's beautiful."

"Probably from the heart outward," Jim said thoughtfully.

Alex smiled up at his shadowy features. "I'm sure she is. Case really deserves this, you know. For once he can't chase the woman he wants in his arms. I guess Sister Theo is a real neat lady. Maybe she'll keep him in line over there." Alex giggled.

"Speaking of neat things," Jim said as he pulled Alex to a halt at the door, "I have a surprise for you."

Alex tilted her head. "Oh?"

"I just received a call from a Major Kean." His hands tightened on Alex's small shoulders. "The appeals board rescinded the charges against me, honey."

It took a moment for the information to sink in. Then Alex gave a cry and threw her arms around Jim. "Oh! Wonderful! Oh, Jim!" she sobbed.

Shutting his eyes, Jim held Alex tightly against him, hearing his voice crack with emotion as he said, "Major Kean said I'd be given corporal status and get all my back pay, plus my benefits from the GI Bill."

Tears glittered in Alex's eyes as she lifted her head to see the relief mirrored on Jim's face. In that moment, she began to realize how much of a silent load he'd been carrying. "And your discharge?" she quavered.

"Medical," he whispered. Framing her face, he drowned in her sparkling gray eyes. "I'm free of everything, Alex!" Then, more softly, he added, "Except I'll never be free of what I did to Kim...to her family. I'll always try to atone for that...."

"You do every day," Alex said brokenly, "and in so many ways." She knew in her heart that Jim would always carry the guilt of his decision regarding Kim. There was nothing to be done about it, except to live with the knowledge and feelings. There were times she saw the haunted darkness come back to Jim's eyes, and Alex knew that he was back there, reliving the atrocity that war had faced him with. And when those anguished moments claimed him, Alex would simply hold and rock him.

Reaching up, she cupped his cheek with her hand. "This is going to be the most wonderful Valentine's Day we'll ever have," she said.

Leaning down, Jim placed a long, tender kiss upon Alex's lips. "All I want," he told her thickly, "is you, and our future together."

Holding him as tightly as she could, Alex nodded, words impossible at the moment. With time, after her father heard about the appeals board overturning the decision against Jim, she knew he would call her. As she felt Jim's arms tighten around her, his face buried against her, Alex smiled softly. "Our life is going to have its ups and downs," she said, "but we love each other, darling."

"And love will pull us through," he agreed, kissing her for a long, long time.

* * * * *

Silhouette Special Edition

salutes

MOMENTS OF GLORY

from Lindsay McKenna

In a country torn with conflict, in a time of bitter passions, these brave men and women wage a war against all odds... and a timeless battle for honor, for fleeting moments of glory, for the promise of enduring love.

February: RIDE THE TIGER (#721, $3.29) Survivor Dany Villard is wise to the love-'em-and-leave-'em ways of war, but wounded hero Gib Ramsey swears she's captured his heart... forever.

March: ONE MAN'S WAR (#727, $3.39) The war raging inside brash and bold Captain Pete Mallory threatens to destroy him, until Tess Ramsey's tender love guides him toward peace.

April: OFF LIMITS (#733, $3.39) Soft-spoken Marine Jim McKenzie saved Alexandra Vance's life in Vietnam; now he needs her love to save his honor....

Silhouette Special Edition ®

You loved the older sister in
The Cowboy's Lady
You adored the younger sister in
The Sheriff Takes a Wife
Now get a load of the brothers in
Debbie Macomber's new trilogy.

continuing with May's
tender tale of love for a

STAND-IN WIFE

When Paul Manning's beloved wife died, he was devastated. But raising three kids alone left little time for healing... until his lovely sister-in-law, Leah, appeared and brought calm to his household. At first it was for the children—for the memory of her sister—then... gradually, magically, unashamedly... for the love of Paul.

Look for the third book of Debbie Macomber's THOSE MANNING MEN in July in your local bookstore.

Take 4 bestselling love stories FREE

Plus get a FREE surprise gift!

FREE GIFT OFFER

To receive your free gift, send us the specified number of proofs-of-purchase from any specially marked Free Gift Offer Harlequin or Silhouette book with the Free Gift Certificate properly completed, plus a check or money order (do not send cash) to cover postage and handling payable to Harlequin/Silhouette Free Gift Promotion Offer. We will send you the specified gift.

FREE GIFT CERTIFICATE

ITEM	A. GOLD TONE EARRINGS	B. GOLD TONE BRACELET	C. GOLD TONE NECKLACE
# of proofs-of-purchase required	3	6	9
Postage and Handling	$1.75	$2.25	$2.75
Check one	☐	☐	☐

Name: _____

Address: _____

City: _____ State: _____ Zip Code: _____

Mail this certificate, specified number of proofs-of-purchase and a check or money order for postage and handling to: HARLEQUIN/SILHOUETTE FREE GIFT OFFER 1992, P.O. Box 9057, Buffalo, NY 14269-9057. Requests must be received by July 31, 1992.

PLUS—Every time you submit a completed certificate with the correct number of proofs-of-purchase, you are automatically entered in our MILLION DOLLAR SWEEPSTAKES! No purchase or obligation necessary to enter. See below for alternate means of entry and how to obtain complete sweepstakes rules.

MILLION DOLLAR SWEEPSTAKES
NO PURCHASE OR OBLIGATION NECESSARY TO ENTER

To enter, hand-print (mechanical reproductions are not acceptable) your name and address on a 3"×5" card and mail to Million Dollar Sweepstakes 6097, c/o either P.O. Box 9056, Buffalo, NY 14269-9056 or P.O. Box 621, Fort Erie, Ontario L2A 5X3. Limit: one entry per envelope. Entries must be sent via 1st-class mail. For eligibility, entries must be received no later than March 31, 1994. No liability is assumed for printing errors, lost, late or misdirected entries.

Sweepstakes is open to persons 18 years of age or older. All applicable laws and regulations apply. Sweepstakes offer void wherever prohibited by law. Prizewinners will be determined no later than May 1994. Chances of winning are determined by the number of entries distributed and received. For a copy of the Official Rules governing this sweepstakes offer, send a self-addressed, stamped envelope (WA residents need not affix return postage) to: Million Dollar Sweepstakes Rules, P.O. Box 4733, Blair, NE 68009.

✂ SS1U

ONE PROOF-OF-PURCHASE
To collect your fabulous FREE GIFT you must include the necessary FREE GIFT proofs-of-purchase with a properly completed offer certificate.

(See center insert for details)